CHABLIS AND LYNTON
IN
THE ROOM OF DOOM

BY

J. WAYNE FRYE

(The retelling of a famous mystery
with a modern twist.)

.

Chablis and Lynton in the Room of Doom

<u>TO: GAY</u>
**You gave me more than you will ever know,
as we shared interludes that brought me
comfort in times that were far too fleeting.
You were a grand and glorious part
for a short time in a life that is filled
with so many fond memories. Thanks for one
of the fondest memories of all.**

And as always, to my muse - Lynton

Copyright 2015 by J. Wayne Frye

This is a work of fiction. Any similarity to persons
living or dead is coincidental.

Catalogue Number: 2014-2453575

ISBN: 978-1-928183-21-1

Fireside Books – Victoria, British Columbia
Part of the Peninsula Publishing Consortium

Chablis and Lynton in the Room of Doom

Author with the Real Lynton Viñas | **About the Author**

Wayne Frye's *Aaron Adams, Girl* series books and *Lynton* adventures are popular with mystery readers. He provides satirical political commentary to many Canadian newspapers, and his books on politics have created a great deal of controversy.

He has written marketing/advertising textbooks, been a highly successful U.S. university hockey coach, professor, university president and served as a marketing consultant to hockey teams and motion picture companies. He has been cited for his work with inner-city gang kids in Los Angeles and been active in the anti-globalization movement. He became a Canadian citizen in 2003 and lives in Ladysmith, British Columbia and Laguna, Philippines.

Other Books by J. Wayne Frye

Hockey Mania and the Mystery of Nancy Running Elk
Something Evil in the Darkness at Hopkins House
How Hockey Saved a Jew From the Holocaust:
The Rudi Ball Story
Fighting for Justice in the Land of Hypocrisy
The Girl Who Stirred up the Whirlwind
The Girl Who Motivated Murder Most Foul
The Girl Who Said Goodbye for the Last Time
Fall From Apocalypse
Armageddon Now
Worth
When Jesus Came to Jersey as the Son of Thunder
When Jesus Came to Canada to Lead an Indigenous Rebellion
Canadian Angels of Mercy – Nurses in Times of Peril
Points of Rebellion: Aboriginals Who Fought for Justice
Lynton Walks on Water
Lynton Curls Her Hair
Lynton and the Vampire at Taygaytay Manor
Lynton Buys a Cell-Phone and Hears the Voice of Doom
Lynton and the Ghosts at the Mansion on Balete Drive
Chablis: Avenging Angel for the Forgotten
In the City of Lost Hope
Chablis and the Terrorist
Who Resurrected the Spirit of Che Guevara
Pursuit
The Disappearance
The Real Jesus as Seen by the Resurrected Spirit of Dixon Frye

J. Wayne Frye

PROLOGUE
HOW DOES ONE DEFINE BEAUTY

The beauty of a woman
Is not in the clothes she wears,
The figure that she carries,
Or the way she combs her hair.
Allure is more than looks.
The beauty of a woman is in her eyes,
Because that is the doorway to her heart,
The place where genuine love resides,
Beauty is the caring that she lovingly gives,
The passion that she shows.
And the beauty of this kind of woman
With passing years only grows.

How does one define a beautiful woman? Most men who say they would be between the ages of 18 and 30, but in reality, at any age a woman can be beautiful. Many women in their 70's exude an intensity of gorgeousness that can put an 18 year woman to shame. A beautiful woman produces this stunning effect because she is the literal embodiment of the human ideal. When you see a truly beautiful woman, you briefly experience a hint of humanity's greatest potential. A beautiful woman is life, not in the sense that she is the meaning of life, but that she is the embodiment of life, the most utterly pure and concrete form of the abstract notion of what it means to be alive. It is an almost mystical experience to look upon true beauty that is manifest from within. Beauty is not just outer looks that titillate a man's libido. Rather, it is something that comes from deep within and rises to the surface in splendorous enrichment that makes the eyes cloud up with wonderment that something so lovely can grace the earth. A beautiful woman can be, literally, down-right intoxicating.

Two women who represent the very epitome of beauty are Lynton Globa Viñas and Chablis Louise Chavez (pronounced Sha-blee). Their personalities and hearts match their appearance. Though they are both in their 30's, their beauty has no age limit as gazing upon them makes a person realize their beauty is timeless. Ironically, while the two of them may fret over lines and wrinkles, those things, for them, are simply confirmation of their beauty, as like their intellects, their beauty is maturing.

Age does not alter that special beauty so many women have. There may be wrinkles, there may be sags, but that sweet glow, that inner light which sparkles like a twinkling star on a cloudless night will forever shine its light that makes certain women achieve immortality with their beauty, no matter their age. Lynton and Chablis are two such women.

J. Wayne Frye

CHAPTER 1
HEELS FROM HELL BY HER SIDE

They are four hot girls in a cold world.
Tender succulent lips are ruby red.
All the men say, "They're beautiful."
But these four can spit red hot lead.

With skills like a surgeon,
These girls can really operate,
While men breathe heavily in awe,
These four march toward their fate.

Look out; they have each other's backs.
In their arms you'd love to dwell,
Because their bodies are like TNT
That makes a man hotter than hell.

You're feeling naughty with your body,
Now spiralling totally out of control.
How'd you like one of 'um in the dark,
A little kiss would make you feel whole.

Yes, these are hot girls in a cold world.
Men for them hunger with desire.
But men should know one hard fact,
These girls can burn you like a wild fire.

Men just desire to be kissing.
They want to move in for the kill.
These girls with bodies so hot
Simply want let men's libidos be still.

J. Wayne Frye

Chablis and Lynton in the Room of Doom

It is hard for men to stay calm,
As they want to make love all day.
But men are so damn naïve,
'Cause these four won't give the O.K.

They are four hot girls in a cold world.
They are packing love's hot fire,
Prancing in those spiked heels,
Here are four hot girls to admire!

It is not often you see four of the hottest women around together at a Manhattan eatery. Chablis Louis Chavez was meeting her three friends from the Philippines for lunch. Lynton Viñas, like Chablis, was well-known, not as a detective like Chablis, but as a renowned demon fighter in her native Philippines. Lynton's two friends, Channa and Ingrid, were with her on vacation visiting Channa's mother who lived on Park Avenue. They had all worked with Chablis in the Philippines on a case dealing with the famed Manila Aswang that had terrorized the Metro Manila area for a year, and as they sat reminiscing, they were interrupted by Chablis' partner Aaron Adams.

"Sorry to interrupt your lunch," said Aaron, "but Chablis I have to go to New Orleans right away to work on the Martinez case. I just wanted to drop by and let you know. I could have called, but then I would not have gotten to see your lovely companions, and it is always a delight to gaze upon these beautiful women."

J. Wayne Frye

Chablis and Lynton in the Room of Doom

The girls all laughed and Lynton said, "Well, it is always nice to be called beautiful, but I am afraid we pale in comparison to your gorgeous partner here."

Aaron smiled as he said, "Yeah, but I get to see her almost every day. I need fresh eye candy."

They engaged in small talk for awhile, but Aaron was in a hurry and had to rush to the airport. The girls continued their leisurely lunch, but what was looming on the horizon would make this one of Chablis and Lynton's last chances at relaxation and frivolity.

It is not without a certain emotion that I begin to recount here the extraordinary adventures of these two women. Yes, I have written of them before, but none of their past adventures reached quiet the level of intensity that they experienced in the manner of this latest in a long line of exciting detecting escapades. I once imagined that the public would never know the whole truth of the prodigious case which I am about to recount here, but my desire to detail it was recently resuscitated contrary to Chablis' decision to simply forget it despite the fact that the entire city, indeed, the entire country and even many foreign countries, were fascinated with a problem that challenged the perspicacity of the police and taxed the conscience of profound thinkers. The solution of the problem baffled everybody who tried to find it in a dramatic turn of events that captivated and fascinated all who knew of it.

Herein, I am merely transposing facts well after the fact, so I can now, with additional documentation; throw new light on what transpired. I do not know what, in the domain of reality or imagination, one can discover or recall that is comparable, in its mystery, with the natural mystery of what I am calling the *room of doom*. Chablis and Lynton were discoverers, after the fact, which delivered the key that unlocked the door to a most perplexing mystery. What I am revealing here is coming out for the first time; because neither woman revealed the whole truth out of fear some innocent party might be injured. They may both decide I abused our friendship by revealing what I am herein, but the entire world was mystified, and I think it incumbent upon me to make it clear how these two women, intelligent beyond compare, responded that very day to what they overheard at the table behind them when someone they did not know rushed in and said "That frightful crime committed at Cornwall-on-Hudson at the house of Nobel Prize winner, Ferdinand LaBoche, will never be solved."

Chablis, curious, turned and said to the man relating the story, "I do not intend to be rude, but your excited manner made you a bit loud, so I overheard the story. I have read about it. Do you mind if we listen, too?"

Chablis and Lynton in the Room of Doom

What man would turn down a beautiful woman like Chablis? Anyway, he immediately recognized her and said, "I know you – Chablis Louise Chavez, right?"

"I am she, sir, and who might you be?"

"Ah, you probably know me by my by-line. I have written of you a few times. I am Conrad Warren of the *Times*."

"I do indeed and thank you so much. You have certainly helped out business – mine and my partner, Aaron Adams."

He and his friend swivelled full around to face her and the one who had rushed in said as his friend looked at the other three girls there, "and you are the dynamic dynamo – Lynton Viñas, the girl with the high heels from hell that dispatched the evildoers in Tagaytay." Then he smiled as he looked at Channa Mendis and continued, "You are Channa, beauty pageant sage who brings grandeur, elegance and eloquence to any runway." Then his eyes twinkled as he offered an assessment Ingrid could have done without. "And you are Ingrid, who seems to always be picking the wrong man."

Chablis invited Warren and his friend to their table. They moved their plates over and thus began the tale that would mystify and titillate the furtive minds of these four women.

Chablis and Lynton in the Room of Doom

As only a writer can, Conrad Warren began to weave his tale of mystery. "On that night, while LaBoche was working in his laboratory, Gay, LaBoche's daughter, who was also his assistant, who was sleeping in the downstairs bedroom next to the laboratory, was ruthlessly assaulted. These two, as you probably know were very famous, as he had said that his Nobel was hers as well as his, since she had always been his trusted right hand. Now, the two were working, at this time, on the theory of dissociative matter – a theory destined to overthrow from its base the whole of official science, which based itself on the principle of the conservation of energy."

"As I am sure you are aware Chablis, as the following day the newspapers were full of the tragedy, but the details were as follows: The state of the victim, Gay LaBoche, made it impossible to get any information from her lips, and the authorities could not form the least idea of what had passed in that place they were now referring to as the *room of doom*. Ms. LaBoche was found lying on the floor in the agonies of near death completely comatose. I have interviewed the assistant, Daniel Jacques, as he was there at the time it occurred, and his bedroom was above Ms. LaBoche's. The laboratory is actually separate from the main house on the sprawling estate, but he has his own kitchen and sleeping quarters above the lab, and was the only one with whom I have been able to talk so far."

J. Wayne Frye

Chablis and Lynton in the Room of Doom

"It was about fifteen minutes past midnight, according to Jacques, who was cleaning and putting instruments in order at the end of the evening's work and was waiting for Mr. LaBoche to go to bed. Ms. LaBoche had worked with her father up to midnight; when she bade the two men goodnight and she went to her room, which was beside the laboratory, and she double-locked the door. There was a moaning; no an intense screeching of a cat that was noticed as the two men heard that dead bolt close on the door. Jacques remembered the moaning cat because he thought it would probably keep them awake all night. I only mention the cat Chablis, because I know you are meticulous in your desire to know great detail in regards to everything that occurred before, during and after a crime. Now, this servant lived in those quarters, because Ms. LaBoche was always there during the warm months, and her father did not want her left alone."

Ms. LaBoche liked it better than the main house as she did not enjoy mingling with all the callers her father had. But she usually returned to the main house in winter as the laboratory is very cold from November until March due to a lack of good heat. There is a fireplace in the laboratory, but not one in Ms. LaBoche's room. However, this particular winter, she had elected to stay right where she was for some reason. Mr. LaBoche and the servant heard absolutely no noise whatsoever from the bedroom where she lay. It was very quiet and the eeriness actually was noticeable the servant said later. He related that LaBoche was seated at his desk, and he was sitting on a wooden chair, having finished his work. It is of great importance that both men were completely quiet and not talking; for, because of that, the intruder certainly thought that they had left the place. And, suddenly, while the old cuckoo clock in the outside hallway was sounding quarter after midnight, a desperate clamour broke out in Ms. LaBoche's bedroom. It was her voice pleading for help. Immediately afterwards, revolver shots rang out and there was a great noise of tables and furniture being thrown about, as if in the course of a struggle, and again the voice frantically cried out for help."

"The two men quickly sprang into action and ran to the room, but it was locked on the inside. They tried to force the door open to no avail. The cries from her for help continued. The two men were overcome with emotion, and kept pounding with shoulders on the door, trying to force it open."

"Suddenly, Jacques had an inspiration that the culprit must have gotten in through the bedroom window. He rushed outside, but because of a narrow alleyway, it was impossible to squeeze through it and get to the window as no more than a mere length of the normal hand separated the first metre of the back wall of the laboratory from the stone wall that went all around the estate."

Chablis and Lynton in the Room of Doom

Chablis was intensely clinging to every word uttered as was Lynton since their furtive, ever alert, inquiring minds were constantly looking for challenges.

Warren was enjoying spinning the tale as he could tell it was generating intense interest. He continued. "To get up to the window one has first to go outside the estate wall. Jacques ran towards the gate and, on his way, met John Brenner, the gate guard and his wife, who had been attracted by the pistol reports and by the desperate cries from the lab. In a few words, they were told what had happened, and Brenner directed Jacques to follow him and his wife to the door in the outside wall. It took them a couple of minutes before they were all at the entrance behind the alleyway."

Stopping, Warren drew on a napkin the exact layout.

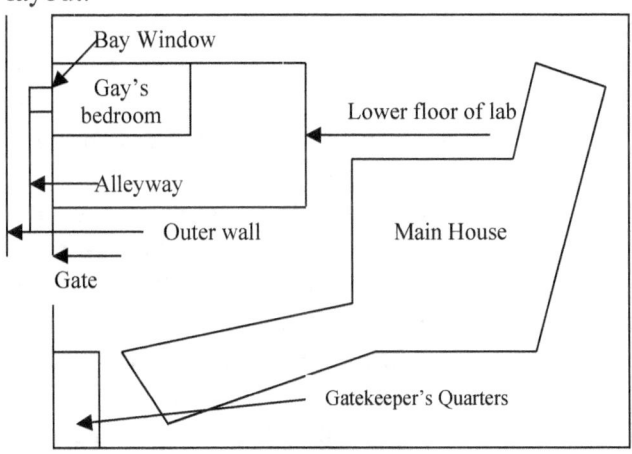

"To their shock, when they managed to finally get to the window, it was locked securely from the inside. Not only were the bars locked, but the blinds inside of them were drawn tight. The intruder, therefore, could not have passed either in nor out that way; but neither could anyone else. While all this was going on outside, Ferdinand LaBoche was still frantically and ferociously trying to break the door down. So, the door of the room was locked on the inside and the window also fastened on the inside; and she had ceased calling for help. She was dead, they all surmised. Still, her father continued to try and break down the door."

"The others returned and all three of the men began to ram the door furiously. Unlike modern homes, this one did not have hallowed core doors but rather they were made of solid oak. Finally, it gave way. Gay was lying there on the floor in the midst of the greatest disorder. Tables and chairs had been overthrown, showing that there had been a violent struggle. Gay had certainly been dragged from her bed. She was covered with blood and had terrible marks of finger-nails on her throat, the flesh of her neck having been almost torn by the nails. From a wound on the right temple, a stream of blood had run down and made a little pool on the floor. When LaBoche saw his daughter in that state, he threw himself on his knees beside her, uttering a cry of despair. He ascertained that she still breathed. Meanwhile the others searched for the wretch who had tried to kill her, but there was no one, absolutely no one else in the room."

Warren looked directly at Chablis. "So, it passes all imagination. The girl is transported to the hospital where she has never regained or probably ever will regain consciousness, so she can offer no help - nobody under the bed, nobody anywhere. All that was discovered were traces, smeared blood-stained marks of a man's large hand on the walls and on the door; a big handkerchief red with blood, an old cap, and many fresh footmarks of a man on the floor, footmarks of a man with large feet whose boot-soles had left a sort of moist black dirt impression. How had this man gotten away? How had he vanished? Don't forget that there is no chimney in the room. He could not have escaped by the door, which is narrow, and on the threshold of which someone always stood. The door, which had been forced open against the wall, could not conceal anything behind it, as all present assured themselves. By the window, still in every way secured, no flight had been possible."

Chablis said, "There were shots fired. Was a revolver found?"

"Yes, it belonged to Jacques. So, maybe the intruder had first gone upstairs to Jacques room which is where his revolver was. Obviously, Jacques was accounted for, so he was never under suspicion in any way, at least at this time."

Chablis and Lynton in the Room of Doom

Lynton said, "How many shots fired, again?"

"Two," said Warren as he raised his right hand, scratched his forehead and Chablis noticed a bandage on his wrist.

"And no fingerprints?"

"Right," replied Conrad with assuredness and then he continued, "All wiped clean, smeared." So, Chablis, I know you and Lynton here have worked together before. What do you say if I can get the paper to hire you to look into this case? If we could publish the solution, it would be a major journalistic coup."

Chablis leaned back in her chair and said, "I fear that the mystery which surrounds the abominable crime will never be brought to light; but it is to be hoped, for the sake of our human reason, that the examination of the walls, and of the ceiling which I shall undertake with the approval of the police department might provide some enlightenment. For the problem is this: we know by what way the assassin gained admission, as he entered by the door and hid himself under the bed, awaiting Gay LaBoche. But how did he leave? How did he escape? If no trap, no secret door, no hiding place, no opening of any sort is found; if the examination of the walls, even to the demolition of the lab does not reveal any passage, if the ceiling shows no crack, if the floor hides no underground passage, one must really believe in the supernatural," and she then looked at her companions as she continued, "and that is where my friends, the demon hunters, come in. Sure, I will look into it with due diligence. Standard daily fee with a bit extra for my friends. Agreed?"

"I will get approval today."

Chablis turned to her friends and said, "So, what do you say girls? Ready to solve a baffling case? You in?"

Channa said, "We may have to pass, as Ingrid and I agreed to take my mom to Vermont."

"No problem. Have a good time," replied Chablis as she looked at Lynton.

Lynton, smiling, said, "I'm in."

Meticulously pouring over the case files and notes, Chablis and Lynton, noticed that particular attention for some reason was paid to the wailing of the cat at the witching hour. Why was that so important? Cornwall-on-Hudson was a rich enclave, but it was also known as a bastion of old-time religion where the many servants who cow-towed to the rich attended fundamentalist churches that thrived and dotted the landscape just outside the affluent area. Perhaps it was encouraged by the rich so those who toiled for meagre wages in the palatial estates would be promised their after-life reward in those heavenly streets that were paved with gold. How ironic that in the United States of America, even the after-life is based on greed, as the streets must be gold to make heaven seem worthwhile. Yep, Americans actually believed Jesus was a capitalist who saw greed as an enviable trait.

Lynton eased back in her chair and said to Chablis: "The devil seems to be on someone's mind here for some unknown reason. There seems a supernatural element implied. Do these people think that a wailing cat was a premonition of evil?"

Chablis, snickering, replied, "Figuring out the American people is a puzzle I will absolutely never solve. Logic and America are polar opposites I have found in all my years here. Wave the flag, shout Jesus and throw in a little devil and you have them in the palm of your hand. They live in a fantasy world where everybody is out to get them and take away all that freedom they are deluded into thinking they have."

Lynton found a rather innocuous item that appeared in a footnote and pointed it out to Chablis: *The landlord of the Dinwiddie Inn explained that the cry of the cat was particularly sinister sounding, like the whine of the famed banshee of Cornwall-on-Hudson.*

J. Wayne Frye

Chablis and Lynton in the Room of Doom

"So, obviously some of these people still believe in evil banshees roaming the countryside," said Lynton.

Knowing Lynton was a recognized expert on the supernatural, Chablis asked with sincerity, "Where does the legend of the banshee come from anyway?"

"Banshees have been around for thousands of years, according to legend. Truth is that the legend evolved from the rich people who actually hired mourners for their funerals. The original banshees were female spirits in Irish lore. They were women who were particularly good at crying, and they were seen as an omen of death and a messenger from the underworld. It is a fairy woman who begins to wail if someone is about to die. In Scottish mythology, she is usually seen washing the bloodstained clothes or armour of those who are about to die. Alleged sightings of banshees have been reported all over the world. Now, why something evil must be female is very interesting as it was assumed that the female of our species carried evil as a result of original sin by Eve in the Garden of Eden." Lynton looked directly at Chablis, gave her a big smile and ended abruptly by saying, "Now you would be an expert on sins of the flesh, so I'll stop here."

Chablis and Lynton had strengthened their ties by coordinating efforts in New York and the

Philippines over the years. They had known each other only three years and the better they got to know one another, the more their affection grew. However, they were two distinct personalities. Chablis was straight forward and in-your-face; whereas Lynton was more tactile and reserved. And when it came to beauty, both shined like a grand beacon of womanhood, but Chablis' sensual attributes were more blatant with an air of wantonness that was never subdued. Lynton, on the other hand, though blessed with a killer body, was much more reserved in her manner, but, of course, innate sexuality cannot be masked when it is natural as it was with her. As her boyfriend Wayne said, "Baby, you are hot and don't even know it."

Together, these two dynamic examples of latent sensuality were about to undertake a baffling case which was to rank as one of the most perplexing in the annals of crime detection. You could almost cut the delight they were experiencing with a knife so intense with interest were they.

The two, worn out from a long day, parted ways, but the next morning, Lynton showed up at Chablis' ready to tackle the case with gusto. As Chablis was walking around topless, as she had no shame; Lynton said to her, "So, what shall we call this accursed room in a mystery that will, no doubt, lead to your biographer and my dear boyfriend, Wayne, to write a book about it?"

Chablis and Lynton in the Room of Doom

Chablis, pouring coffee, said, "Conrad Warren has already given us the name for it. We shall call it the case of the *room of doom*."

They both laughed and Lynton said, "I don't much believe in intruders who make their escape through walls of solid brick. I think Jacques did wrong to leave behind the weapon which became part of the crime that was committed and, as he occupied the attic immediately above her room, the old blueprints I ordered this morning will give us the key of the enigma and it will not be long before we learn by what natural trap, or by what secret door the intruder was able to slip in and out without detection. Of course, at this point everything is hypothesis not fact."

Chablis, pointing at the kitchen table for Lynton to have a seat, sat down opposite her and offered an observation. "No trap door will be found, and the mystery of the room will become more and more perplexing. That's why it interests me. The examining magistrate is right; nothing stranger than this crime has ever been known in the annals of detecting."

"Have you any idea of the way by which the intruder escaped?" Lynton asked.

"None," replied Chablis, "none, for the present. But I have an idea as to the revolver; the intruder did not use it."

"What? I don't understand."

Chablis sighed. "It was used by Ms. LaBoche. Very ineffectively I might add."

Lynton, a light seemingly going on in her head, said, "Of course, you brilliant detective you. The intruder strangled her, ripped at her body furiously. He had no desire to use a gun, but what of the locked door?"

"That's the real conundrum in the whole case as far as I can see right now with only a cursory examination. Of course, the whole situation is truly baffling."

"O.K., but what about the bolt being locked? Ms. LaBoche took extraordinary precautions! It is clear to me that she feared someone. And obviously you assume she is the one who used the revolver and took it from Jacques without telling him. No doubt she didn't wish to alarm anybody, and least of all, her father. What she dreaded took place, and she defended herself. There was a struggle, and she used the revolver skilfully enough to wound the killer in the hand I assume, which explains the impression on the wall and on the door of the large blood-stained hand of the man who was searching for a means of exit from the chamber. But she didn't fire soon enough to avoid the terrible blow on the right temple as mentioned in the medical report. Am I right?"

Chablis and Lynton in the Room of Doom

"Yes."

Lynton shifted positions in her chair and sat up straighter as she said, "What of that blow to the woman's temple?"

"The blow on the temple seems to show that the intruder wished to stun his victim after he had unsuccessfully tried to strangle her. He must have known that the attic was inhabited by Jacques, and that was one of the reasons, I think, why he must have used a quiet weapon."

"All that doesn't explain how the intruder got out of the room," Lynton observed.

"Evidently," replied Chablis, rising, "that is what has to be explained. I am going to the LaBoche home now. Let me put on a dress and we are off."

Chablis received a generous retainer from the newspaper by courier right before they left. She told Lynton half of it was hers, but Lynton just shrugged her shoulders and said, "Whatever is fine."

Chablis did not realize it until they were introduced, but she had actually met LaBoche once before at a Hunter College reception. He remembered her and said, "I can understand why you would forget me, but a beautiful young woman like you is hard to forget." Then he turned to Lynton and said, "And now, I have two beautiful women to remember." Just as he got the word "remember" out, he broke down and started crying, realizing that he would never see his beautiful daughter conscious again.

Chablis said, "It is O.K. to cry."

Local constable, Merlin Melson, had been summoned by LaBoche to meet the two women there, as it was assumed that he might have some cogent insights to what occurred. Melson walked with them to Ms. LaBoche's bedroom, which had not been touched since the investigation. Mr. LaBoche could not bear at the moment to go with them as he said the pain was unendurable. Chablis walked around the room several times, pausing often to scan all about. She was precise and meticulous in her observations.

Melson said, "So, what you think Chablis?"

"Difficult to assess obviously, but I see several signs of what indicates a very precise attempt to throw investigators off the scent with what is a series of very clever ruses. This is no ordinary intruder, no run-of-the mill perpetrator. This is a wily, committed and devious individual who has a very definite purpose. What that purpose is I cannot deduce at this point, but we are dealing with a highly intelligent individual who actually is probably secretly enjoying the way he has baffled the authorities. It is as if he is playing mind games with the authorities, enjoying seeing us so confused and bewildered. There is still a method to all this though – a method that will take a grand effort to uncover. This guy is every bit as fiendish as Professor Moriarty, and though I am no Sherlock Holmes, I firmly intend to give this miscreant a run for his money. As Holmes would have said, 'the game is afoot.' I look forward to the challenge."

Melson said, "And you think this man has indicated what?"

"I think if he isn't a man in high society, he is, at least, a man belonging to the upper class as defined in this country, which means probably part of the arrogant, bombastic, self-absorbed, greedy 1% at the top of the economic ladder. But that, again, is only an impression. I see no facts to support the contention at present. That is more intuition than good, solid detective work. However, my intuition is based on my detecting skills, so I think it highly likely I am right in my assumptions."

"What has led you to form that impression of his station in life?"

Chablis looked over at Lynton and made a motion with her right hand, indicating Lynton should explain. Smiling, Lynton said, "Well, the greasy cap found at the scene, the common handkerchief that was on the bed, and the marks of the rough boots on the floor. All items purposefully placed here in this room to throw the investigators off the trail. Intruders don't leave traces behind them which tell the truth. Those items were left to indicate some poor robber had broken in, not someone of affluence. Still, he is, no doubt, worried about Ms. LaBoche regaining consciousness, as she might be the only one capable of indentifying him; although, the doctors' prognostications indicate that is highly unlikely to ever occur."

Chablis nodded her head affirmatively. In Lynton, she had an investigative partner every bit as observant and intelligent as she was. It was a pleasure to have the dynamic dynamo with the heels from hell by her side.

CHAPTER 2
DECEPTIVE OBVIOUS FACT

Two with brains and beauty
Tread where others won't go.
Together these determined girls
Will forcefully lay evil low.

Watching a beautiful woman is a grand adventure, but watching two is a double treat for the eyes. These two women strolled past people like shadows of glory as their beauty was playing a symphony of delight in Cornwall-on-Hudson. Male and female alike were captivated by Chablis' confident stride as her perky little braless breasts bounced delightfully in what seemed synchronized perfection. Lynton's primary asset (how is that for a pun) was her curvaceous ass that wiggled provocatively like moulds of Jell-O being placed on a table for dessert. Oh, and what a dessert. Those morsels of delightful flesh were as soft as a cloud floating across a purple sky above an azure blue sea with waves gently undulating as if whispering "dive-in, dive-in."

The first stop was the Town Court, where the District Attorney was talking about his previous nights sojourn to Manhattan where he attended an off-Broadway play. (Who can afford anything but off-Broadway nowadays?) The play was at the Parisian and was by an unknown calling himself Rene Minaldo. According to the DA it was well-worth the $50 ticket price and would get this new playwright, who had apparently never been seen by anyone, an offer for Broadway.

When Chablis approached the District Attorney, he was delightful and gregarious, even saying, "Know you girl. I read the *Times* and I have seen you splashed across the front page a few times. And who is this Asian woman with you, another P.I.?"

"She is from the Philippines. This is Lynton Viñas," said Chablis.

"Robert Bowman, District Attorney, here, what can I do for you ladies, today?"

"Interested in the LaBoche case," replied Chablis.

Throughout his magisterial career, Bowman was especially interested in cases capable of furnishing him with something in the nature of a drama. Though he might very well have aspired to the highest judicial positions, he had never really worked for anything but to win a success at the Cornwall-on-Hudson judiciary. Because of the mystery which shrouded it, this case was certain to fascinate so theatrical a mind. It interested him enormously, and he threw himself into it, less as a magistrate eager to know the truth, than as an amateur of dramatic imbroglios, tending wholly to mystery and intrigue, who dreads nothing so much as the explanatory final act. For him, the pursuit of a solution was more important than the solution itself.

Bowman offered an immediate assessment of the situation at the LaBoche estate. "I talked to Detective Melson about what you deduced from yesterday's cursory investigation. I have sounded every single wall and examined the ceiling and floor and I know all about it. I am not to be deceived, Ms. Chavez. Now, I am no slouch when it comes to investigations, but I know you are one of the best. What you think? How'd he get out?"

"We are still assessing things. We've had a look, but have only some preliminary ideas at this particular point – most perplexing situation it is."

At that moment, the person to whom Bowman had been enthusiastically speaking, said "I am Ronald Means, local journalist. So, you think this will ever be solved."

Chablis smiled at him. "Can't say for sure right now. Some cases are never solved. So far I have been very fortunate and never had one that was unsolvable, but there is always the first time for everything."

It was then that Chablis decided to show Means what a good detective she was. Smiling, she said,

"You were the writer of the play Mr. Bowman saw last night."

"What? How, how did you know that? There is only one person in the whole world besides me knows. It is impossible to know that, impossible I tell you."

Still smiling, Chablis said, "I'm a trained detective."

Lynton then decided to deflate Chablis' ego a bit just for fun, when she offered an explanation to show Chablis that she was not the only smart detective there. "Mr. Means, there are a couple of give-ways. When you were listening to Mr. Bowman talk about how good the play was, your interest peaked up immediately. You even puffed out your chest a bit indicating that there was some hidden pride when you heard how much Mr. Bowman liked the play. Then there was the name of the playwright, Rene Minaldo – same initials as Ronald Means. The paper in your hand is turned to the play reviews section, and when we walked in, we both heard you asking if the play was good and you had a tinge of excitement in your voice, obviously you wanted a friend's favourable comments. Then, there is the bag you are carrying with a book in the outside pocket just peeping out enough to make out that it is entitled *The Playwrights Guide to* something as the rest of the title is hidden under the flap."

J. Wayne Frye

Chablis and Lynton in the Room of Doom

Chablis got a big smile on her face as Lynton looked at her. Chablis said, "A few more weeks with me, and Lynton will be more in demand than I am."

Lynton, shrugging her shoulders, said to Means, "So, the pseudonym is to protect your job and to avoid any recriminations if the play had failed."

"Right you are little lady. You two girls are something else. Never seen any two sharper minds," said Means.

Chablis offered her observations as she laughed out loud. "Be damn hard to find. That's for sure."

"I hope I can rely on all of you to not reveal what you know."

They all enthusiastically agreed to keep Means' secret, and at Mr. Bowman's insistence, they all went back to the LaBoche estate.

Bowman said as he drove them all to the estate. "An unbelievably incredible unfathomable case, and my dear Ronald there is only one thing I fear, that as a journalist you will be trying to explain it or attacking us for being unable to explain it."

"I shall do neither Robert. I will report the facts as they are, and as for speculation, I am too baffled to do any of that."

Chablis and Lynton in the Room of Doom

Robert said to Means, "You will have to stay in the car, because LaBoche has given strict orders – no press allowed in his home as he has had bad experiences with them so far."

Bowman turned to Chablis, who was riding up front with him, and said, "Have you met Gay LaBoche's boyfriend Raymond Marquet?"

"No."

"I assumed you had not, so I called ahead and asked that he be here. Thought it might be of interest for you to meet him. Poor Raymond, this dreadful affair has made him so morose, as he is so deeply in love with Gay LaBoche. His sufferings are truly painful to witness. Then there is Mr. LaBoche, if she does not recover, it will not be long before he is in his grave. What an incalculable loss to science his death would be!"

Lynton chimed in, "But Ms. LaBoche is not dead. May she not survive?"

"Doctors say there is no hope of her ever regaining consciousness, and have asked Mr. LaBoche to pull the plug, but he simply cannot bring himself to do it. She is dead, but only breathes as a result of the ventilator. Disconnect it and she is gone."

"Horrible situation," offered Chablis.

J. Wayne Frye

Chablis and Lynton in the Room of Doom

Lynton said very forcefully, "A serious wound to the temple like she has generally means irreversible brain damage of the most serious kind, but there have been people who miraculously survived, even people who have been in comas for over 30 years and amazingly and unexpectedly come out of them."

Chablis said, "Anyone have an idea what was used to deliver the blow?"

"Absolutely not," replied the two men simultaneously, but Bowman's reply was tacit as if he was obviously holding something back.

Chablis' mind was beginning to race through the facts. She asked, "The room has but one barred window; the bars of which have not been moved, and only one door, which had to be broken open and the intruder was not found?"

Bowman replied, "That's so."

Those wheels were turning in Chablis' head even more prodigiously and rapidly now. "How did Gay LaBoche wear her hair on that evening?"

Looking at her intensely puzzled by the obtuse question, Bowman said quizzically as he reached down in the cubby hole and handed her the file. "Don't know what difference that makes. Here is the file. See for yourself."

Chablis and Lynton in the Room of Doom

Chablis gazed over the file with great intent. "The way the hair was worn is important," she said. "I see here that she had her hair drawn up in a knot on the top of her head. I wonder if that was her usual way of arranging it with her forehead completely uncovered.

"Injuries are often the result of incredibly simple things that are easily overlooked," interjected Lynton.

Bowman said, "I can completely assure you, for the medical examiner has carefully examined the wound. There was no blood on the hair, and the arrangement of it has was not disturbed when she was treated in the main house by paramedics and removed from the scene."

"You are sure that on the night of the crime she did not have her hair in bands," asked Chablis.

"Quite sure," the DA replied.

"A pity she had her hair drawn back from her forehead. If she had worn it in bands, the blow she received on the temple might have been weakened."

"The wound was extremely bad, I assume" said Lynton.

"Horrible, but hardly visible."

Chablis and Lynton in the Room of Doom

Lynton sarcastically said,, "You know what weapon was used to deliver the blow?"

"I am bound by good reason not to reveal that. I am sorry," replied a surprised Bowman.

Lynton, every courteous in manner replied, "We understand. Can you tell us if you have found the weapon?"

He simply did not answer, which the two women took to mean either they did not know what the weapon was or that he was not at liberty to reveal what it was. It was O.K., as it was often deemed prudent for law enforcement to withhold some facts in order to trip up any potential suspects.

Chablis said, "And the wound on the throat?"

Here, Bowman readily confirmed the decision of the doctor that, if the murderer had pressed her throat a few seconds longer, the woman would have died of strangulation.

Lynton said, "Can you tell us, Mr. Bowman, if you are aware that the shots were fired by Ms. LaBoche, not the intruder."

"Please," he surprisingly replied, "call me Robert. And you two are very very good. Yes, I deduced fairly soon that it was not the intruder who fired the shots but Ms. LaBoche. Haven't revealed that though. The door in the vestibule is the only direct entrance to the lab, a door always automatically closed, which cannot be opened, either from the outer area or inside, except with the two special keys which are never out of the possession of either Mr. Jacques or Mr. LaBoche. Gay LaBoche had no need for one, since Jacques lodged above the lab and because, during the daytime, she rarely left her father. When they all rushed into her room, after breaking open the door, the door in the vestibule remained closed as usual and, of the two keys for opening it, Jacques had one in his pocket, and LaBoche had the other. As to the windows, there are four; the one window of the room itself and those of the two in the laboratory looking out on the countryside and the window in the vestibule looking into the back yard. There is also a small window in the attic."

"So, he would have had to leave by a window then," said Chablis, "as the only door to the outside was locked just like Ms. LaBoche's room door. My guess is the vestibule window."

"Yes," offered Bowman, "but how did he get to that window from the locked room?"

Smiling, Chablis said, "That, my friend, is the mystery and why we are here."

Bowman said, "But why do you assume he left by the vestibule window?"

"Why? Oh, the thing is simple enough! As soon as he found he could not escape by the door of the place his only way out was by the window in the vestibule, unless he could pass through a grated window. The window in Gay LaBoche's room is secured by iron bars and the two windows of the laboratory have to be protected in like manner for the same reason. As the intruder got away, I conceive that he found the only window without bars that of the vestibule, which opens on to the back yard. That is the only logical answer."

"But that vestibule window, though it has no bars, has solid iron blinds and is kept closed most of the time," said Bowman.

Chablis said, "I took careful note of looking at the pics of the crime scene and the iron blinds were obviously fastened by their iron latch; and yet I saw traces of blood on the inside wall and on the blinds as well as on the floor, and footmarks to attest to the fact that the intruder obviously made his escape by way of that window. But then, how did he do it, seeing that the blinds remained fastened on the inside? He passed through them like a shadow. But what is more bewildering than all is that it is impossible to form any idea as to how he got out of that room unseen in the first place. That is the real mystery here."

"Could that window have been closed and refastened by the intruder?" asked Means.

"That is what occurred to me for a moment; but it would imply an accomplice or accomplices, and at this point, I am not ready to say he had an accomplice," interjected Chablis.

Finally, all but Means, exited the car. They were told by the maid that Mr. LaBoche was weary, and simply could not be disturbed. Chablis, Lynton and Robert asked to go out to the lab. They were given the key after she procured it from LaBoche.

"Let us go into the attic," said Chablis, and they ascended the spiral staircase into a dusty place where, had someone been up there, large footprints would have been left in the thick dust which filled the floor. The only footprints were those of Jacques who had very large feet and probably Gay's due to their size. There was a skylight that looked onto the countryside but it was barred. The blinds on the one window, which naturally open inwards, had not been unfastened. They went back downstairs in a very casual manner. Again, it appeared to all three that the would-be assassin had escaped through the vestibule window somehow. "The revolver, obviously, was not a totally successful deterrent for Ms. LaBoche, but based on the blood, she must have been able to shoot him at least once," offered Chablis.

Pointing, Bowman said, "I am sure you noticed one bullet was embedded in the wall stained with the impression of a red hand, a man's large hand and the other in the ceiling."

"Yes," said Chablis. "The wall makes sense, but the ceiling is curious."

"Why curious?" replied Bowman.

"She would have had to fire it lying down aiming upward toward the ceiling. Doesn't usually happen. Can't remember it ever happening."

Thinking for awhile, Bowman said, "Not in my experience either – never, in fact." then, obviously curious at Chablis' take on things, he continued, "then you do think there were accomplices?"

"I am not sure, but I have suspicions. Tell me, did you know Ms. LaBoche?"

"No, never met her, but know of her. She was considered a noble woman and never let her station in life go to her head from what I heard."

Lynton, smiling, said, "Well, she must have been incredibly brave to face-off against an intruder the way she did," and looking over at Chablis, grinned broadly and continued, "Especially because of the bullet in the ceiling."

Chablis saw Lynton was toying with her and let the comment slide. Asking to stroll about the grounds, Chablis went outside with Lynton and Bowman. Built originally in the heart of the forest, gradually other homes were constructed around the estate. Chablis wandered outside the gate and started looking around the area. There was a mass of inharmonious structures, dominated by the tall steeple of a church in the distance. Good place for a church thought Chablis as these rich people have a lot to be thankful for, and, no doubt, the church took in a tidy sum every Sunday from people who loved to be seen in all their finery.

It was in this place where Mr. LaBoche and his daughter settled to be away from prying eyes, but gradually, civilization crept up around the estate where father and daughter had installed themselves to lay the foundations for the science of the future. Its solitude, in the depths of woods, was what, more than all else, had pleased them. They would have none to witness their labours and intrude on their hopes, but the aged stones and grand old oaks. Still, the immenseness of the estate kept the closest neighbours at least a half a kilometre away. This land, of present mournful interest, had fallen in disarray, owing to the negligence of two people who were single-minded in the pursuit of scientific endeavours. The laboratory alone, which was hidden from street view, had preserved traces of strange metamorphoses over the years as modern accouterments had been added, like iron bars on the windows. Such was the chateau in which science had taken refuge, a place seemingly designed to be the theatre of mysteries, terror, and probable death of the most insidious kind.

Chablis quizzically said, "What of Mr. LaBoche. Tell me about him and how he came to buy this place."

"It had for a long time been unoccupied. Another old chateau in the neighbourhood, built in the 19th century, was also abandoned, so the area had a dearth of homes. Some small houses on the side of the road leading from town, an inn, called the Dinwiddie, were about it at the time. The deserted condition of the place had apparently been the determining reason why the LaBoche's chose it. He had just left Harvard, as had his daughter, where their work had made a great stir. The book which he had published, on the *Dissociation of Matter by Electric Action*, had aroused interest from the U.S. government and many scientists throughout the world. He inherited a great fortune from a distant uncle. This fortune was a great boon to him; for, though he might have made millions of dollars by exploiting two or three of his chemical discoveries relative to a new process of dyeing, it was always repugnant to him to use for his own private gain the wonderful gift of invention he had received from nature. He considered he owed it to mankind, and all that his genius brought into the world went, by this philosophical view of his duty, into the public lap rather than for personal gain. This was not at all pleasing to the corporations that had feverously bid for his patents."

Lynton interjected, "So, he was altruistic in every sense of the word?"

"Yes, very much so. He did not try to conceal his satisfaction at coming into possession of this fortune, which enabled him to give himself up to his passion for pure science, he had equally to rejoice, it seemed to him, for another cause. His daughter, when he bought the estate was only 20 years old, and had graduated with a Ph.D. from Harvard at that young age, as she started university at 14. She was exceedingly beautiful. She was said to look like her mother who had died upon her birth. Twenty years of age, a charming blonde, with blue eyes, milk-white complexion, and radiant, Gay LaBoche was one of the most beautiful marriageable girls in all of New York State. Yet, she seemed only concerned with helping her father. So, they buried themselves in their work. People felt him selfish, but his daughter told everyone that her first love was her father and then her second was devotion to her work. She was singularly minded for the most part, but, of course, did, on occasion avail herself of male companionship.

"So," said Chablis, "she was content here at this place?"

"She was. It can be said without hesitation that her incredible passion for science lead her so far as to refuse all the suitors who presented themselves to her for over fifteen years. So secluded was the life led by the two, father and daughter, that they showed themselves only at a few official receptions and, at certain times in the year, in two or three friendly drawing-rooms, where the fame of the professor and the beauty of Gay made an incredible sensation. The young girl's extreme reserve did not at first discourage suitors; but at the end of a few months, they tired of their quest."

Chablis said, "But apparently one suitor was successful in wooing her."

Bowman replied, "One suitor persisted with determined tenacity. Raymond Marquet was much older than she, fifty to be exact and she thirty-five. He persisted in his pursuit, even though she had made it plain that she would never marry."

"Suddenly, some weeks before the events with which we are occupied, a report - to which nobody attached any importance, so incredible did it sound - was spread about town, that Gay had at last consented to crown the inextinguishable flame of Raymond Marquet! One day, Ferdinand LaBoche, as he was leaving the Academy of Science, announced that the marriage of his daughter would be celebrated in the privacy of the chateau as soon as he and his daughter had put the finishing touches to their report summing up their labours on the Dissociation of Matter. The new household would include Raymond Marquet, who was himself a scientist of some renown. The scientific world had barely had time to recover from the effect of this news, when it learned of the attempted assassination of Gay LaBoche under the extraordinary conditions which we now explore."

Lynton, always quick to assess a situation, said, "And now we enter the scene like interlopers in the sands of time. One thing I have found out in all my adventures is that there is nothing as deceptive as an obvious fact. Somehow we are missing what is probably as obvious the nose on our faces."

J. Wayne Frye

CHAPTER 3
CALM BEFORE A BREWING STORM

In that valley of doubt,
Souls of hope are
Like animals in a slaughter house
Hanging there on hooks.

This is the place of doubts;
The garden of good and evil.
There is a death weapon,
Though no one is dead.

A body lingers in a coma,
The smoke of question
Permeates, slowly rising.
This is the room of doom.

There is the smell of doubt.
Sunlight dances in blades.
Intruder escaped in haste,
Or was it methodically planned.

Did he pierce like an arrow?
Did he cut the night air
Like an invisible knife
Through the darkness?

Is the intruder a phantom
That lurks still about
While these two detectives
Are in determined pursuit?

Chablis and Lynton in the Room of Doom

Scrounge all about.
This is a mysterious estate,
Where the intruder vanishes
Like a vapour into thin air.

Chablis is Holmes.
And Lynton is Watson.
These two lay the seeds
Where a solution sprouts.

Chablis was persistent in the need to question Mr. LaBoche further, so they all gathered in the living room where news of his daughter was not good and he came into the room reluctantly when summoned by the DA. No doubt, being rich, his daughter was getting the very best of care in a nation where only those at the top of the economic ladder were afforded the finest medical care in a system, like everything else in the country, which was based on the profit motive. Still he agonized.

Chablis and Lynton noticed that most of their queries were being evaded by LaBoche. They looked at one another quizzically, as they were both of the opinion that he was hiding something.

It was not long until Robert Marquet showed up to inquire about Gay, and Lynton and Chablis began to question him. Could it be possible that he was somehow involved in the whole mysterious affair? Then again, almost anyone could be involved.

J. Wayne Frye

Chablis and Lynton in the Room of Doom

Each minute, each hour made things more perplexing. Neither woman could find an explanation as to how the intruder had been able to leave the room. Along with that mystery, which appeared to me so inexplicable, remained the absolute dearth of a specific suspect. Chablis and Lynton thought it was best to refrain from suspecting anybody. But, then, a seemingly senseless phrase from Marquet played upon Chablis' mind. He said, when talking to LaBoche, "The laboratory has lost its charm, and the garden outside the entrance all of its brightness. It is as if Gay is never returning."

There was finality to the way Marquet said it, and based upon the prognostications of Gay's doctors, he was probably right, but there was something in the way he said it. As the group sat down, Lynton motioned for Chablis to come over by the window that looked out on the grounds. She whispered something, and then Chablis turned toward those in the parlour. "Have any of you an idea how the shots were heard all the way down at the Dinwiddie Inn? It is almost 2 kilometres away. It seems strange they could hear a shot that far away, and they also mentioned the cat howling?"

"There seems no explanation," replied Marquet as Jacques walked in and was introduced to Chablis and Lynton by LaBoche. He was a bit austere looking, but extremely distinguished with his thick white hair and somewhat stiff bearing.

Lynton turned toward LaBoche, "And the two owners of the Dinwiddie, they actually showed up here? Am I right in that regards?"

"Yes."

"And they were both very distressed, assuming the worst?"

"Yes, they were," offered LaBoche.

Lynton was in deep thought now as she said, "So, they heard the shots. What time was it they heard the shots?"

LaBoche replied, "They said it was exactly 12:15 AM as they looked up at the clock behind the bar when they heard the shots."

"And they got here when?" interjected Chablis.

LaBoche blurted out, "It was 12:19, as Jacques, my assistant glanced up at the clock in the lab when he went to open the outside door."

Lynton, her mind calculating furiously now, said "So, two kilometres is about 1.3 miles. This man and woman, who are not that young, ran less than a 4 minute mile then, assuming the two clocks were exactly the same in their time. Maybe they should try out for the Olympic team. They had time to cover so great a distance as that which lies between their lodge and this place, in the space of four minutes. Suspicious I say, unless the clocks were indeed not synchronized in time. Obviously they must not have been."

LaBoche took a deep breath and said, "They were exactly the same. They looked at a computer clock on the cash register they said, and I was working on my computer, so I looked at it as well as heard the cuckoo clock in the vestibule. I can assume that the times were exactly the same on both computer clocks as they are set by impulse and are very accurate"

Lynton continued her train of thought. "That is what is so incredible. They were here so quickly and then there is the fact they heard the shots and the cat. O.K., we are going to run a little experiment. Do you have another gun in the house?"

LaBoche shook his head no as did Jacques. Chablis looked directly at Lynton and said, "You know I am packing."

Lynton said, "Hey, this is the United States of America isn't it? Is it not logical to assume everyone is packing?"

Chablis smiled, reached down and raised up her dress, exposing her magnificent right thigh as she pulled out her snub-nosed .38 from the thigh holster. She started to hand it to Lynton, but Lynton pointed at Jacques, as she wanted no part of firearms. Chablis handed it to him and said, "Fire it into the ground outside the window of Gay's room in 30 minutes. I will be at the Dinwiddie to see if I can hear it."

Chablis walked into Dinwiddie with a regal like stride and everyone there, men and woman, stared at her intently, because they were simply not used to seeing such a beautiful woman, She sauntered up to the bar where the two proprietors stood in awe. The woman said, "Yes, can I help you ma'am?"

"Sure, I'll have a seven and seven and light on the ice."

The man behind the bar, Mr. Lorton, kept staring at Chablis as if she were an illusion. She had two drinks and stayed about forty minutes. She walked out much to the dismay of the men there who were all panting like dogs waiting for their dinner. She arrived back at the chateau and shrugged her shoulders when they all looked at her. No, she had heard no shots.

Lynton said, "They lied. There is no doubt about that. They must have been already waiting, not far from the house, waiting for something! Certainly they are not to be accused of being the authors of the crime, but their complicity is not improbable."

J. Wayne Frye

Chablis and Lynton in the Room of Doom

Chablis offered her take on things. "I am not sure what to think. It is baffling to say the least. All options are on the table as of now. The trouble is I don't know what the options are."

The two women asked and were given permission to roam about the estate. They walked outside. The towering oaks there were centuries old and stood majestically all about. Autumn had already shrivelled their tawny leaves, some of which had fallen onto the ground. There was an intense loneliness to the place. They walked all around the estate, then stood in front of the laboratory and stared at the doorway in the darkness that surrounded them. The little door alone marked the entrance to the laboratory. It looked like a tomb, a mausoleum of sorts. It was eerie and foreboding.

As they came nearer the door, they both felt trepidation. The building was ominous looking as the lone outside lamp about 100 feet away cast an eerie glow on the entrance - a narrow heavy faded bronze coloured door with a huge latch on it.

The place had a ground-floor which was reached by a few steps, and above it was an attic where Jacques stayed. The plan of the ground-floor consisted of the room where Gay had been assaulted with its one barred window and one door opening into the laboratory. Then was the laboratory with its two large barred windows and its two doors, one opening into the vestibule, the other into Gay's room. The vestibule had one unbarred window and the door opening to the outside, a bathroom off the right and stairs leading to the attic room where Jacques slept. And there was a chimney in the laboratory right next to Gay's bedroom.

How then, thought both ladies, did the intruder escape from the room? Chablis walked back to the three steps at the entrance to the building. She turned to Lynton and said, "What do you think was the motive for the crime? Do you have any ideas at all?"

Lynton tilted her head, sighed and said, "The nails of Gay's fingers, the deep scratches on the chest and throat show that the wretch who attacked her attempted to commit a frightful crime that almost smacks of passion." She then seemed to be in deep thought for a few seconds before continuing. "The medical experts, as we have reviewed the files, could not affirm that the marks were made by the same hand as that which left its red imprint on the wall; an enormous hand it was though, much larger than is the norm for a man. Maybe a crime of passion, but I doubt it."

"Could not that blood-stained hand have been the hand of Gay, who, in the moment of falling, had pressed it against the wall, and, in slipping, enlarged the impression?"

J. Wayne Frye

"According to the report, there was not a drop of blood on either of her hands when she was lifted up," replied Lynton.

"Yes, and we know that it was Gay who was armed with Jacques's revolver, since she apparently wounded the hand of the man who assaulted her. She was in fear, then, of somebody or some thing."

Lynton replied, "Yes," as she moved toward a small spot on the floor, bent down and stared intently.

Chablis said, "What is it."

Lynton replied as she picked up the little piece debris and sniffed it, "It is a piece of ham I'd say. Yes, a piece of ham, no doubt about it. How could the forensic guys miss this? Pretty shoddy work I would say."

"Yes," offered Chablis as she moved toward the wall by the headboard of Gay's bed.

Lynton saw exactly what she was looking at and said, "More malfeasance," as Chablis bent over and picked up a small white fragment of something.

Chablis, holding the tiny fragment up, said, "I know what the weapon that hit her head was."

Chablis and Lynton in the Room of Doom

Lynton said, "You are holding a bone fragment, right?"

Smiling, Chablis said, "The weapon was a ham bone. Probably a very large ham bone."

There, standing in the doorway was Robert Bowman. "I hoped to keep it a secret, but you ladies are too smart, and, of course, the forensic guys are dumb for leaving debris around. My guess is you two astute detectives would have figured it out anyway."

Chablis said, "Then you have the ham bone that was used in the attack?"

"We do. However, I beg you not to say anything as it is our ace-in-the-hole. Only we three and the forensic experts know about it. It was an enormous bone, the top of which, or rather the joint, was slightly indented, probably from the frightful wound. It was an old bone, which may, according to appearances, apparently have been used to bludgeon something previously."

"You sent it off for analysis," said Lynton.

"To the lab in Albany, yes. However, the Medical Examiner thinks he has detected on it, not only the blood of Ms. LaBoche, but other stains of dried blood, evidence it was used in a previous crime or crimes."

Chablis and Lynton in the Room of Doom

"If a below were delivered properly," said Chablis, "it could be as deadly as a hammer."

"According to the M.E., the wound would have been mortal, if the blow had not been arrested in the act by Ms. LaBoche. Still, considering she is in what the doctor's say is an irreversible coma, I suppose one could consider it a mortal blow."

Chablis said, "So, wounded in the hand, he dropped the mutton-bone and fled and Gay was stunned after having been nearly strangled. If she had succeeded in wounding the man with the first shot of the revolver, she would, doubtless, have escaped the blow with the bone. But she had certainly employed her revolver too late; the first shot deviated and lodged in the ceiling; it was the second only that took effect."

He replied, "Yes, absolutely correct are your assumptions."

Jacques walked in like an ill-wind at the close of a day. He said, "Guess two will-o-the-wisp detectives from New York City can solve the unsolvable?"

Jacques actually cut a dashing figure for a man his age. As mentioned previously, a beautiful head of thick white hair, a neatly trimmed white beard, and he had an usual gait as he walked about, scanning the room with great intensity as if he expected something to be there. Each step seemed overly deliberate, as if he was trying to avoid stepping on something in the room. He was immaculately attired with coat, starched white shirt and tie. His shoes were so meticulously shined that they sparkled in the glistening light of the full-moon that filtered into the room. His eyes were dark and intense. Chablis replied to his comment with, "Ah, Mr. Jacques, you seem to look upon us as interlopers, not two people trying to help find the person who attempted to murder your employer's daughter?"

"I see no reason why you are any more skilled than the local constabulary."

Lynton said, "We may not be any better, just different with a different perspective. I am sure you are anxious to find the culprit."

Without hesitation, he said, "Of course."

Lynton, in a slightly perturbed voice, said, "Could you tell us how Ms. LaBoche wore her hair the night of the assault?"

"She wore it as she always does – loose and slightly drawn up so that," and here he paused a second or two as in deep thought before continuing, "her beautiful forehead could be seen, pure as that of an unborn child! Gay was perfection. Yes, perfection of the most beautiful kind. Everything about her was - I mean is perfection personified."

Chablis pointed outside the room and motioned with her head for Lynton to follow. In fact, all in the room walked out into the vestibule. Robert Bowman, taking extreme notice of the lean, but muscular legs displayed by Chablis, could not help but sigh as he realized this was perhaps the sexiest woman he had ever encountered. Chablis' very manner bespoke a woman with no inhibitions. One who could offer a man incredible delights in the embrace of desire.

Chablis walked over to the vestibule window, Robert enthralled with her gently swaying hips, said, "What is it?"

"Jacques comments. He is in love with Ms. LaBoche."

A note of recognition in his eyes, Bowman said "My, my, oh my. Yes, you are right. It was obvious in the way he described her - if not love, then fascination for sure."

"No, it is love," she said as she looked at Lynton and continued, "We women know the difference between love and lust, though they are often intertwined in the grand and glorious chase between man and woman, or man and man or woman and woman."

Chablis and Lynton in the Room of Doom

Jacques came out into the vestibule, and as he did, Bowman, to avoid his assessment of what they were discussing, said to Chablis as he pointed at the vestibule window, "Ah, the window from which the culprit made his escape."

Jacques, shaking his head furiously, offered his assessment. "Poppycock. If he had gone off that way, we should have been sure to have seen him." Then he looked directly at Robert and said, "Why have they not arrested me Mr. Bowman on account of my revolver? I am sure you know it was unregistered and thereby in violation of the handgun act."

Robert said, "I wouldn't worry about it. I am sure you will be contacted in regards to that, but no one is usually put in jail, only fined."

Chablis, uninterested in the illegality of the gun, asked Jacques as she was fidgeting with the shutters on the window in the vestibule. "Were the shutters closed at the time of the assault?"

"Fastened from the inside as they are now."

Turning to Robert, Chablis said, "Any blood stains found outside?"

Momentarily, interrupting his intense survey of Chablis' beauty, he replied, "Yes, near the foot stones under the window."

Chablis and Lynton in the Room of Doom

"And the ground was moist that night, so there were some footprints in the ground?"

"No, none the size of those in the bedroom."

Jacques interrupted vociferously, "The intruder did not go this way."

Lynton said, "Oh, really? So you have assessed the situation and concluded that?

"I have."

Slightly grinning, Lynton said, "Which way did he go then?"

Shrugging his shoulders, he replied, "How the hell do I know, but he couldn't have gone this way, though - impossible."

Chablis and Lynton looked at one another, and then dropped to their knees. As they did, Robert was thinking how he would love for Chablis to drop to her knees in front of him. He was actually titillated by the thought of sex with a transsexual as beautiful as Chablis.

Ever astute to assessing a situation, Lynton, as they were on their knees whispered to Chablis, "You have yourself an admirer."

Chablis whispered back, "I know."

As the two continued to look about while on their knees, Jacques, in a very irritated manner, offered his unrequested assessment: "You will find nothing I tell you. And now it is all dirty; too many persons have tramped over it. On the day of the crime I had washed off the walkway and stones with a high powered hose. They would have also been damp with the night mist, so there would have been tracks left. None, none were found leading away from here. They just abruptly stopped," he said as he glanced over at Robert, who shook his head to affirm what was said.

"Interesting," said Chablis. "Marks in her bedroom left on the floor but none here."

Lynton said to Jacques, "Did you make it a habit to wash the walkway regularly?"

Seemingly offended, Jacques barked, "I do my duty. I keep the place around the lab spic and span, the lab too. He would not have crossed this path without some sign being left. Any idiot could deduce that. It doesn't take a Sherlock Holmes to figure that out. All you had to do was look and they did. Nothing. No prints."

Again, Bowman was nodding his head in agreement. Chablis said, "We know the intruder was wearing boots from the prints in the bedroom. It is true, had he walked across here; there should have been some heavy prints leading away."

Chablis and Lynton in the Room of Doom

Lynton said, "Can you be exact with the time when you washed the stones and walkway?"

"I would say around 5:30. Gay's father always takes a little walk before dinner. It is always around 5:30 when he does. The police came and saw all the marks there were on the bedroom floor as plain as day. There were none in the laboratory nor in the vestibule, which were both as clean as a pin."

Chablis stood and leaned against the nearby tree, scratched her head and said as she moved over to the far side of the window as she looked up toward the attic where Jacques' room was. She pointed at the window in the attic, which had no bars since it was too high to easily access. It was about 5 feet to the right of the vestibule window. She walked over into the bushes beneath it, looked behind them and turned to Robert and Lynton as she pointed downward. They moved toward her and looked behind the bushes. One almost indistinguishable large footprint could be made out in the moonlight behind the bush, almost under the bush itself, obviously made by a large boot. Robert had a look of amazement as he said, "Incompetent. Utterly incompetent."

Chablis said, "Not really that big a deal. I mean how could he have gotten up to the attic room? Could he have cut a hole in the bedroom ceiling and then dropped to the ground outside the vestibule window. I mean that is a drop of a good 20 feet. Anyway," she continued with a smile, "there's no hole in the ceiling of the bedroom. So, we still know nothing of how he got out."

Jacques said, "The devil is at work here."

"Devil?" replied Chablis. "I doubt the devil had anything to do with this any more than God did. This is the work of a diabolical person though. That is for sure."

Lynton who had moved back toward the walkway, slowly but methodically, went inside the vestibule and was on her knees as the others walked back in. She was in front of the bathroom. She was intently examining something as they all stood silent. Looking back over her shoulder, she said to Robert, "The incompetence is pretty glaring." She pointed down at a minute spec right in front of the bathroom door. They all gathered round and with squinted eyes they saw it. There was a drop a blood maybe the size of a pin head. Lynton turned to Jacques and said, "Did you clean up in here that day, before the assault?"

Without hesitation, he blurted out, "I clean everywhere, every day, except since the crime."

Chablis knew exactly where Lynton was heading with her questions, so she asked the of Jacques. "While you were cleaning in the laboratory and this vestibule was the vestibule window open?"

"No, it was not. Definitely not. Wait, wait a minute. Yes it was. I opened both the windows in the laboratory and this one, to make a current of air; then I shut those in the laboratory and left this one open when I went out to wash the walkway. When I returned here, this window had been closed. I assumed Gay or Ferdinand had closed it. I forgot. I forgot. I am sorry. You think, you think he got in then?"

"Maybe, maybe not. We cannot be sure at this point," replied Chablis.

The troop made their way to the laboratory. Lynton's eyes were drawn at once to the door of the bedroom to her left. It had been closed. She looked at the others and said "Did we not leave that door open?"

No one could remember. Shrugging it off, Lynton and Chablis began to scrutinize the laboratory closely. The room was large and well-lit. Two big windows were protected by strong iron bars and looked out upon a wide extent of country. Through an opening in the forest, they commanded a wonderful view through the length of the valley and across the plain to the town of Cornwall-on-Hudson which could be clearly seen in the distance. The whole of one side of the laboratory was taken up with a large chimney, and such implements as are needed for chemical experiments; tables, loaded with phials, papers, reports, and various machines to as Jacques offered "demonstrate the dissociation of matter under the action of solar light." Along the walls were cabinets, plain or glass-fronted, through which were visible microscopes, special photographic apparatus, and a large quantity of crystals. Lynton walked over to a large cubicle and traced the side of it with her right hand fingers. Then, she held the particles up, rubbing her thumb and index finger together. "Something was burned here," she said as she placed the small particles on a nearby piece of paper and handed them to Robert so he could have them analyzed. She then bent down and saw small particles on the floor. She looked to her right where there was a beaker. In the beaker was a small piece of paper, obviously remains of what had been a larger paper that was burned. She picked it up, looked at it and read what she could make out: "Presbytery, lost nothing, charm, nor the garden, its brightness."

Standing there in the doorway was Mr. LaBoche. Lynton said, "You burn this piece of paper?"

"No," replied LaBoche, but there a very deep anxiety in his trembling voice as he looked over with intensity at Jacques who was breathing heavily.

J. Wayne Frye

Chablis and Lynton in the Room of Doom

Chablis and Lynton took careful note of the reaction of the two, as they continued surveying the laboratory. Chablis was examining the chimney which grew narrower towards the top, the outlet from it being closed with sheets of iron, fastened into the brickwork. "Impossible to get out that way," she said, getting up from her knees

Chablis moved to the windows. At the second window Jacques was standing in contemplation. Chablis, very pointedly, said, "And what are you looking for?"

"Just looking at two women who are grasping at straws."

"Well," said Chablis. "Pardon me all to hell for trying to solve the mystery of why your employer's daughter was assaulted and how the culprit might have escaped."

LaBoche said, "Jacques, enough."

He nodded his head and replied. "Sorry miss. Very sorry. I guess I am a bit overwrought with the whole situation."

Chablis could not resist. "It's OK. I'd be upset too if my revolver was involved in a crime."

He straightened up, took a deep breath and said nothing in reply, as Chablis moved toward the door to Gay's bedroom. Standing at the door, she looked back at the people there. Appearing suddenly in the lab doorway was Marquet as she said, "This is like a quiet calm before a brewing storm."

CHAPTER 4
LEVEL WITH US

There are two who never falter in doubt.
They assess all that there is about.
Standing side-by-side they probe the dark
Hear the sullen cry - hark, hark, hark!
Chablis and Lynton clues they devour.
These girls do not fear the witching hour.

Chablis, having pushed open the door to the bedroom, paused on the threshold saying something that will become clear later in this tale, "Ah, the perfume of the lady in black!"

The chamber was dark. Jacques was about to open the blinds when Chablis stopped him. "Did not the tragedy take place in complete darkness?" she asked.

"No, there was a dim light on her nightstand," said Mr. LaBoche almost matter-of-factly. "She had it on every single night."

"O.K.," said Chablis as reach to turn the dim light on.

It did not work, so she kept clicking it off and on. She reached up and unscrewed the bulb, looked at it closely, but it was not burned out. She screwed it back in and tried again. Still, it wouldn't work.

Chablis and Lynton in the Room of Doom

Jacques said, "Want me to get you another bulb? There is one in the hall, or I can turn on the overhead light."

"Is the lamp exactly as it was," asked Chablis.

"Well, it was turned over the night of the crime," interjected Bowman. "We just put it back in position after taking pictures. We never checked to see if it was working,"

Chablis said, "Close the door. I want the room in complete darkness."

Jacques went back into the laboratory, closed the shutters of the two windows and the door to the vestibule. The room was completely dark, pitch black.

Chablis took out her cell-phone, turned on its flash light and placed it on the nightstand. "Is that about the right amount of light?"

Mr. LaBoche said, "Yes."

Chablis asked all of them to step outside as she did, too. They closed the door and waited for awhile. Looking about, they all, except for Lynton, wondered why they were waiting. Lynton, realizing they were confused about what was happening, said, "She is waiting for our eyes to adjust to the light in here, as the night of the crime, the lights in here were on, and it is important that we see the room just as these two did. Just be patient and our eyes will soon be ready to see the room as it was seen that night."

Bowman stood in awe of the two as he said, "I see."

Chablis turned the knob and quickly opened the door. The room was indeed dimly lit, but the dim light of the cell phone made it possible to see all about the room. They could vaguely distinguish objects about the room, especially a bed in one corner, and, in front of them, to the left, the gleam of a mirror on the wall, near the bed. "That will do," said Chablis. "You can open the blinds."

As Jacques pushed open the shutter, the pale light entered from without, throwing a sinister glow on the walls. The wood floor was covered with a single yellow rug which was large enough to cover nearly the whole room, under the bed and under the dressing-table, the only piece of furniture besides the nightstand that remained upright the night of the crime it was revealed. The centre round table, the night-table and two chairs had all been overturned. These did not prevent a minute stain of blood being visible on the mat, made, as Bowman informed them, by the blood which had flowed from the wound on Gay's forehead. Besides these stains, drops of blood had fallen in all directions, in line with the visible traces of the footsteps, large and black, of the assailant. Everything led to the presumption that these drops of blood had fallen from the wounded intruder who had, for a moment, placed his bleeding hand on the wall. There were other traces of the hand on the wall, but much less distinct.

Lynton walked over to where the majority of the fingerprints were. "See this blood? The man who pressed his hand so heavily upon the wall in the darkness must certainly have thought that he was pushing at a door. That's why he pressed so hard. He was confused, disoriented and looking for the door in the darkness. If you follow the trace of the hand, it is evident after leaving its imprint that he sought the door, found it, and then felt for the lock as the pattern moves with intent toward the door."

Looking over at the door, Chablis said to Bowman. "My guess is there was no blood on the door or the door knob?"

"Correct," replied Bowman.

Jacques said, "What does that prove? He might have opened the door with his left hand, which would have been quite natural, his right hand being wounded."

"He didn't open it at all!" LaBoche exclaimed. "There were four of us when we burst open the door! He could not have gotten by us."

Chablis and Lynton in the Room of Doom

Lynton walked over to the hand prints and said, "The pattern shows a purpose."

"Yea," interjected Chablis. "He was actually drying his hands on the wall. He had no towel, and apparently decided that rather than use the bed sheets, the wall was a proper way to dry the blood off, or maybe he wanted his prints there."

Placing herself next to the wall, Lynton, who was 5:2, but 5:5 in her heels, stood on her tiptoes to reach the stain. Looking over at Chablis, she said, "probably about 5:8, maybe 5:9."

Looking up at the bullet hole in the ceiling, Chablis said, "The shot was fired straight, not from above, and consequently, not from below. It is almost as if the gun were purposefully aimed at the ceiling."

Lynton walked to the door and carefully examined the lock and bolt, satisfying herself that the door had certainly been burst open from the outside, and, further, that the key had been found in the lock on the inside of the room. She finally satisfied herself that with the key in the lock, the door could not possibly be opened from without with another key. Having made sure of all these details, she let fall these words: "That's better!" She then took off her heels, placed them by the door and walked quietly into the other room with no fanfare.

She then walked back into the bedroom, and surveyed it meticulously. She stood in silence as did Chablis. Lynton smiled at Chablis and said as she looked at Jacques, "And what time Jacques did Mr. and Ms. LaBoche arrive at the laboratory?"

"I don't know. I guess about 6."

Then she looked over at Mr. LaBoche, and he replied "Yes, that is right."

Lynton lay down on the floor and looked under the bed. "Here it is. He was definitely under the bed. You can see a slight intention in the room rug under the bed. I assume no one thought to look examine the indentation here."

LaBoche, excitedly said, "We did. Under the mattress there was nothing but the metal netting, which could not conceal anything or anybody. Remember that there were three of us and we couldn't fail to see everything, the room is so small and scantily furnished."

"How was she taken from this room?"

"Jacques carried her to the main house."

"Not a wise move for an injured person. I am surprised Mr. LaBoche that you would not insist she not be moved until the paramedics arrived."

J. Wayne Frye

LaBoche, stuttering, said, "I, I guess I was not thinking."

Lynton said as she was still peering under the bed, "The mattress has been moved slightly. It is not squarely on the frame. The top is off just a bit, but there is no dust, so it was sitting there before."

Jacques offered an explanation. "We might have moved it a bit when we were looking under the bed for the person. We did peer under it as you are doing. When we could not find the culprit, we wondered whether there was not some hole in the floor.

Chablis interjected, "So, there is no cellar, but you still thought there might be a door in the floor?"

LaBoche said, "Yes, we, I mean I knew there was no cellar, but we were not thinking rationally I guess."

Chablis looked determinedly at Jacques. "Why would you be the one who removed her from here?"

Jacques look at her quizzically, but did not answer. He just ignored the question. However, Chablis knew the answer and so did Lynton, but they were not prepared to reveal it at that particular time.

Chablis and Lynton in the Room of Doom

Bowman offered a further clarification of things when he blurted out. "We looked under the bed intently as part of the investigation, despite there being no cellar. It is just unfathomable how he managed to get out."

Chablis paced the four corners of the room, so to speak, sniffing and going around everything almost like a blood hound, surveying all that she could see, which was not much, and everything that she could not see but was obviously formulating in her head.

Lynton literally passed her nose and hands along the walls, constructed of solid stucco. When she had finished with the walls, and passed her agile fingers over every portion of the yellow wallpaper covering them, she reached to the ceiling, which she was able to touch by climbing on a straight-back chair she pulled from the far corner, and by moving this ingeniously constructed stage from place to place as she examined every foot of the ceiling. When she had finished her scrutiny of the ceiling, where she carefully examined the hole made by the bullet, she approached the window, and, once more, examined the iron bars and blinds, all of which were solid and intact. At last, she gave a grunt of satisfaction and declared "absolutely incredible."

Chablis said, "It is sealed as tight as a bank vault."

Chablis and Lynton in the Room of Doom

Lynton suddenly whispered, "Quiet. Quiet. Do you hear that?" She stretched her arm toward the wall at the back of the room, near the window.

Jacques suddenly said, as they all heard a low whining as if someone was crying. "There, yes, you can hear it at times. We have all heard it on occasion. It is the crying of the old woman, Ms. Richelieu. She walks to her daughter's tomb in the graveyard near the estate wall. Sometimes her cat trails her down the road, scurrying along beside her, almost like a dog would."

Lynton and Chablis looked at each other. Chablis said, "No one thought the cat heard might have been the one that accompanies this woman to her daughter's grave late at night? That maybe this woman might have heard or seen something?"

Shaking his head, Bowman said, "She is crazy, absolutely bonkers. You cannot get any sense out of her at all. There is no need to question her I assure you."

Lynton said, "The report said that there was a cap and a handkerchief left here."

"They were," replied Bowman.

Lynton, the wheels of her mind turning like a precision Swiss clock, said, "I have seen neither the handkerchief nor the cap, yet I can tell you how they are made. The handkerchief is a large one, blue with red stripes and the cap is an old Brooklyn Dodgers hat."

Bowman said, "How the hell do you know that?"

Lynton walked to side of the bed, pointed at the night stand and said, "The handkerchief lay here on the night stand. You can see that when it was picked up by the crime scene investigators they left a slight impression on the dusty table at the top and bottom ends where it lay. Size is easy."

"But how do you know it had blue and red stripes," asked Bowman.

Chablis let out a little laugh as she said, "She's just playing with you. That is a guess on her part, but is she correct?"

"Yes. But what about the old Brooklyn Dodgers cap?"

"Well," offered Chablis. "The report said it was an old timey baseball team cap found in the room. My little Ms. Sherlock over there," she said as she pointed to Lynton, "knows a bit about baseball as I take her to Yankee and Mets games often when she visits. She also knows through me that the only two teams from the past that it could be would be the New York Giants or the Brooklyn

Dodgers. Everyone knows that the Dodgers were the most popular team. Just a guess on her part, but a very good one."

Lynton, smiling at Chablis' revelations, said, "Please, you are destroying my mystique here."

The footprints in the room had been left in tact and they had all skirted around them, but now Chablis was a bit more intense in her analysis of them. She took a piece of paper from the nightstand drawer and removed a pair of scissors and bent over the footprints. Placing the paper over one of them she began to cut. In a short time she had made a perfect pattern which she handed to Lynton.

Lynton moved toward the bed again. She stood staring intently as she said, "Women lose about 50 to 100 hairs a day. She then turned to Bowman and said, "How many hairs were removed from the crime scene?"

"Ah, ah I don't know."

"There were some removed," asked Chablis.

"Yes, from the weapon used, and also from the floor beside Gay."

"But not 50 or 100? Those we would find in the bathtub from when she washed her hair, probably earlier in the day as few women wash their hair before going to bed."

"No, not 50 or 100," replied Bowman. "Only a small number, maybe 10 or 12 at the most."

"Please have Mr. and Mrs. Brenner come and meet us outside. Could you do that Mr. Jacques?" asked Chablis.

"Of course. Immediately."

The Brenner's arrived quickly, and Chablis said as they all walked outside to where the footprints were, "So, the night of the crime Mr. and Mrs. Brenner, you were alerted to what happened after the fact."

The Brenner's did not speak, just nodded their heads affirmatively.

"Are the two of you familiar with the woman who occasionally walks nights to the graveyard?"

Mr. Brenner said, "We are, it is nothing unusual though. It happens two or three nights a week ever since her daughter was killed three years ago."

Lynton quickly asked, "How was she killed?"

"Assaulted on the streets one night. Brutally beaten over the head and tossed to the roadside."

Chablis and Lynton in the Room of Doom

Chablis did not have to ask the question. She just looked at Bowman who said, "No, the killer was never caught. No leads whatsoever."

Chablis, looked at the Brenner's and said, "So, what about the cat that is usually with her? Does it ever wail?"

Both shook their heads no, as Mr. Brenner said, "Never heard it do more than meow on occasion, and that rarely."

Chablis said, "So, Gay was taken into the chateau, carried by Mr. Jacques.?"

LaBoche said, "Yes."

"Let's go to the chateau," said Chablis.

Lynton's phone rang as they walked toward the back entrance to the house. It was her boyfriend, Wayne. "Hi baby. What's up? I am in the middle of something right now."

Wayne whispered low. "I just wanted to hear your voice. I miss you."

Lynton whispered in return. "I miss you too, baby.

As they walked inside, Wayne, who always loved titillating Lynton with flowery language, said, "I was born when I saw your pic on Skype. I have lived a few years in blissfulness since you said you loved me. I only existed before I met you, only existed not lived until I held you in my arms."

Lynton, noticing everyone looking her way, whispered to Wayne. "Not now baby, not now. Everyone is looking at me. Mahal kita (*I love you* in Tagalog)."

Wayne, laughing a bit, loved teasing her and said, "Oh my, I wouldn't want to embarrass you talking about how I want to make passionate love to you. How I want to run my hands up your……"

Just then she forcefully cut him off with, "Bye baby," and quickly disconnected.

Chablis gave her a nondescript wink and suddenly turned toward Mr. LaBoche for the following interrogation:

Chablis: "What did you do on that day of the assault? I want you to be as precise as possible."

LaBoche: "I rose late, at ten o'clock, for my daughter and I had returned home late on the night previously, having had dinner at the Academy of Science of Philadelphia honorarium. We worked together till midday. We then took half-an-hour's walk in the park, as we were accustomed to do, before lunch at the chateau. After lunch, we took another walk for half an hour, and then returned to the laboratory. There we found the maid from the main house, who had come to clean my daughter's room. Gay briefly went into bedroom said hello to the maid and resumed our work after a few seconds. At five o'clock, we again went for a walk in the park and afterward had tea.

Chablis: "Before leaving at five o'clock, did anyone go into your bedroom?

LaBoche: "My daughter went into it, at my request, to get her jacket, as it had grown a bit cool outside and since she is prone to catch colds easily, I suggested she wrap up."

Chablis: "And she mentioned nothing suspicious there?"

LaBoche: "Nothing."

Chablis: "It is, then, almost certain that the intruder was not yet concealed under the bed. When you went outside, do you know if the door of the room was locked?"

LaBoche: "I didn't check, but probably not, as there would be no reason for it to be locked."

Chablis: "You were absent from the place for some length of time, your daughter and you?"

Chablis and Lynton in the Room of Doom

LaBoche: "About an hour probably."

Chablis: (Talking to herself more than to those present.) "It was during that hour, no doubt, that the intruder got in. But how? Nobody knows. A footmark has been seen leading away near the window of the vestibule right under the attic window, but none has been found going towards it. Did you notice whether the vestibule window was open when you went out?"

LaBoche: "I don't remember."

Chablis" "And when you returned?"

LaBoche: "I did not notice."

Chablis: "This is very important. Are you sure you didn't notice? I mean it was right there in front of you almost. Should have been easy for you to see." She then turned toward Jacques and continued, "Would you have opened it while they were out?"

Jacques: "Don't remember. Probably not as there would be no reason to go into Gay's room."

Chablis: "Oh, there was always a reason to go into her room." Smiling, she did not pursue her statement any further, just stared for a second at Jacques and moved on to another topic. "Do you recollect, Mr. LaBoche, if during your absence, and before going out, he had opened it? You returned to the laboratory at six o'clock and resumed work?"

LaBoche: "No, don't recollect, but as he said, there is no reason for him to go into her bedroom."

Chablis: Again, she looked at Jacques as she said. "No reason? Oh, I am not so sure." Again, she left the group hanging as she moved on with another topic. "And neither you nor your daughter left the laboratory after that until she retired for the evening."

LaBoche: "Neither of us. We were working."

Lynton was enjoying the intensity of the questioning, because as she followed it closely she was amazed at the meticulous manner in which Chablis explored every minute detail. She also knew that there was something explosive coming, something she knew and Chablis knew, something that would come as a shock to Jacques and LaBoche.

Chablis: Looking at Lynton as she knew they shared a secret, addressed LaBoche. "Did you eat in the lab?"

LaBoche: "As I said, we were engaged in work, very engaged. We had no time to go back to the main house. So, yes we did."

Chablis and Lynton in the Room of Doom

Chablis: "You regularly dine in the lab?"

LaBoche: "Almost never. I was visited by my gardener whom I told to do certain things the next day, and my daughter called the main house and said we would have dinner in the laboratory."

Chablis: "Could the intruder have known that you would dine there that evening?"

LaBoche: "How could he. We didn't even know ourselves until the last minute."

Chablis: "And it was midnight when your daughter went to bed."

Jacques: I went in and closed her blinds right before she retied."

Chablis: Almost matter-of-factly, Chablis said, "Of course you would do that for her. And you saw nothing suspicious?"

Jacques: "Of course not."

Chablis: "Mr. LaBoche, Jacques was with you afterward the whole time?"

LaBoche: "Yes."

Chablis: "When your daughter entered the bedroom, she immediately shut the door and locked and bolted it? That was taking unusual extreme precautions, knowing that her father and the servant were there? Was there a reason, something that she should fear?"

LaBoche: "It was not normal, no. It was not necessary."

Chablis: "Why would she want a gun?"

LaBoche: "I am not sure, but for several nights, she said she heard unusual sounds, sometimes footsteps, at other times the cracking of branches. I did not pay much attention to it." He then put his head in his hands and with muffled voice, said, "I should have listened to her."

Chablis: She turned to Jacques and was getting ready to drop a bombshell, but decided the time was not yet right, so she would wait a little longer, maybe even let Lynton bring up that which would surprise all there, as she asked, "And did she ever say anything to you about her fears, Mr. Jacques?"

Jacques: He seemed to think for a second. "Yes, she did. I mean she said nothing much, but now I remember she asked me a curious question. I'd forgotten it. She asked me if I still had that old gun by my bed."

Chablis to everyone present: "None of you know of any enemies she had?"

They all shook their heads no. However, Jacques did offer an additional comment. "She had not been her normal self for several days."

Chablis: "Could all of you there see the nightlight glare under the door?"

They all nodded affirmatively and LaBoche said, "The nightlight was burning. No doubt about it."

Looking at Jacques first, then LaBoche, Chablis said, "What was the first indication something was amiss?"

LaBoche: "We heard her cry out, "murderer, fiend."

Jacques: "Exactly."

Chablis: "And there was a great commotion in the room then?"

LaBoche: "Terrible. She was screaming, and we heard two shots fired. We assumed it was the intruder firing at her. I was beside myself with anguish."

Jacques: "Yes, we were frantic with worry for her, absolutely frantic. The commotion only lasted a few seconds, and then the quiet made us even more fearful."

Chablis and Lynton in the Room of Doom

Chablis: "Was the light still on?"

LaBoche: "Yes, yes it was, you could still see it under the door."

Chablis: "And what about a shadow? Was there any diminishing of the shadow at all, as if someone might be walking about inside the room?"

Jacques and LaBoche looked at one another intently, then turned to Chablis at the same time and shouted, "Maybe!" LaBoche stared at Jacques and said, "I'd seen shadows in there before."

Chablis, her dazzlingly voluptuous body moving across the room like a graceful gazelle springing across the plains in the wilds of Africa, sighed deeply as she approached Jacques. Standing before him in her famous high-heels from hell, gazing into his eyes, she very forcefully said, "This has been an interesting interrogation, but you are holding something back. There is something you know about this you aren't revealing."

He stuttered, "How, how, how…"

Chablis, her succulently alluring lips puckering as her mouth opened slightly and she licked the middle of her upper lip exposing the underside of a tongue that, even in this tense situation, caused a stir between Bowman's legs as he observed her confrontation with Jacques and wondered what it would be like to experience duelling tongues with this nubile miss, as she said to Jacques, "Come on Jacques, time to level with us about you and Ms. LaBoche."

CHAPTER 5
A CHANCE FOR EROTIC DELIGHT

Be not deceived by what appears unfound.
What lurks mercilessly in the shadows
Sometimes borders on the profound.

Everyone there, but Lynton, stood in bewilderment at what Chablis had said. Jacques was just staring at her, without uttering a word, so shocked was he. He was actually shaking as Chablis continued, "Level with us about your relationship with Gay. So, you are much older than she, not as educated as she, not as renowned as she. So what? It is nothing to be ashamed of. Lynton loves a man much older than she and more famous than she is. It happens. The most famous country-western singer of all time, Loretta Lynn, was married to an auto mechanic for fifty years."

Jacques put his head in his hands and began to cry. Lynton put her arms around him, and pulled him to her chest as he muttered, "I, I encouraged her to seek another, to find someone more like her, an educated man, a man of distinction. Why, I am nothing, nothing I tell you."

Lynton, very determinedly said, "You are something, Mr. Jacques. You were very important to her, and she to you." Then Lynton turned her head toward LaBoche and said, "And you know of the relationship and disapproved."

Chablis and Lynton in the Room of Doom

LaBoche, dumbfounded, was muttering, "I, I"

"Oh, you cannot figure out how we know? We know because little things about love stand out. They present themselves in the most mundane ways. Jacques here said earlier that Gay asked if he still had the gun by his bed. Well, obviously, Gay had been in his room, likely been in his bed."

They were all shaking their heads now, amazed at the women's perceptiveness. Lynton continued. "As for you knowing of the affair Mr. LaBoche, it was obvious the way you were staring at Mr. Jacques and commenting about the shadow you had seen before, that you were referring to knowing he was in that room with your daughter on occasion."

Bowman was shaking his head now, realizing that in these two women he had the epitome of investigative prowess. They were the modern Holmes and Watson.

Meanwhile, Marquet was reeling in shock, or maybe rage. You could see seething anger within, but shock would have been too strong for the countenance he displayed. Had she told him, or did he just know it from observational analysis.

"Tell me about your affair, Mr. Jacques," said Lynton. "We need no lurid details, just facts as they relate to the case."

Chablis and Lynton in the Room of Doom

He looked over at LaBoche as he said, "It started years ago really. When she was very young, but I did not pursue her interest in me, because I saw her, even in her 20's as a child, as she had been sheltered so by her father. Her life was him and his work. His work was her work, his life hers."

LaBoche took a seat and sighed as it was obviously painful for him to hear that his daughter had sacrificed so much for him, and that even her love of Jacques was sacrificed for his desire to have her marry someone of equal status to her.

"So," said a sympathetic Lynton, "when did your affair begin in earnest?"

Jacques now took a seat too, and with a long sigh and an obviously heavy heart began his story. "She said she loved me right after we moved here, all of us together. I had served Mr. LaBoche at the university, and he graciously encouraged me to come here with them. I am 25 years older than she, and I told her that it would not work because of that. I told her that it was more than the age difference; it would not work because her father, though a man of great compassion and magnanimity in his embracing of those less intelligent, simply would not hear of his daughter marrying a lowly servant. We were from two different worlds. She refused to date anyone else, always telling me that if she could not have me she would have no one. She went to her father and told him of her love. He could have fired me, but he didn't. He is not that kind of a man. He is my friend as well as my employer, but he told me in no uncertain terms that I was to have no romantic relationship with his daughter, absolutely forbid it. I honour him, and respect him, so I fought hard to obey his wishes, so hard."

Lynton said, "And this went on for many years?"

"It did, yes. I did not seek her out. One night right after her engagement to Raymond Marquet, which was forced upon her by her father, she came to my room, simply slipped the door open and standing there in her sheer nightgown, standing there in the moonlight, glowing like an angel, I...." He then looked over at LaBoche and dejectedly said, "Please I cannot continue with Mr. LaBoche here. I do not want to talk of such things about his daughter in front of him."

LaBoche, without a word, got up and walked out of the room, head down, shoulders slumped in dismay. Marquet left with him. Lynton said nothing, only looked at Jacques and with facial gestures bade he continue.

"I am but a man? I may be old, but, as you can tell by my stares at you and Ms. Chavez, I am not dead, and I do still have a functioning libido. I gave into temptation. Do not blame her, she had

J. Wayne Frye

fought her desires for so long, but once she was engaged, she felt the need to finally consummate the love she had for me before subjecting herself to a life with the man her father had picked for her. We began to meet nightly after her father would leave the laboratory. Sometimes in her room, usually in mine, so naturally she became aware that I kept a gun by my bedside. Hey, I'm an American, what would you expect?"

"Go on," said Lynton.

"Well, Mr. Marquet began to occupy more and more of her time, but still she spent almost every night in my arms, often crying inconsolably, saying that she deplored the thought of life without me. That she would not be able to practice fidelity with a man she did not love as long as I was around. I began to contemplate leaving for that reason. I really did. I even inquired about other positions." He put his head in his hands and began to sob. "But how I loved her, how I adored her, how I longed day and night to be in her arms, to feel the warmth of her love. Oh my, I am speaking of her in the past tense," he blurted out as he sobbed uncontrollably. "She is not dead yet, oh please, please if she can only regain consciousness, I will go, go and never look back knowing that she lives."

Lynton stood by his chair, placed her hand on his shoulder and said, "Love is not always a path strewn with rose petals. It is a treacherous and often unforgiving road. Fortunately, I have travelled that road only once in my life, but always know that it is better to suffer pain from love than to have never known love at all. Today, I am loved and adored by a man who himself has endured great pain in a previous love, and together we have found a certain nirvana of hope. I hope that Ms. LaBoche can be restored to health, and if she is, do not hesitate, do not tarry in doubt. Grab love and devour it like it is a great feast. Age, social prominence, economic status be damned."

Lynton felt sorry for Jacques, because he had laid his soul bare with his declaration of love for Gay. They had both built a barrier to forestall that love, because of convention and fear of ridicule as well as a sense of duty to Mr. LaBoche. She placed her right hand on his left shoulder and very quietly and sombrely let him know she understood. "You know, my boyfriend Wayne is much older than I am, and that fact almost kept him from pursuing me. Then, I had also told him that I was not much when it came to sex and that I had actually lost my live-in boyfriend of six years, because I was frankly, not attentive enough for him sexually. I can see in Wayne's demeanour that he is reluctant to make passionate, unbridled love to me, because he feels old and unappealing and thinks that his time for lust has passed him by and that he sees me as being too beautiful to be interested in an old man. The truth is that my interest in him is complete and total, not because of his looks or his prowess as a lover, but because he loves me so much. I feel it in every word, every action. I can see it in his eyes, feel it in his touch, and hear it with his flowery words of affection. I can sense him looking at me in the middle of the night as I lie in bed naked, and sometimes I hear him sobbing, sobbing because he feels so lucky to be loved by me. But the truth is, I am the lucky one, because all my life I have been seeking someone to genuinely love me, and though he is much older than I am, in Wayne I have found unconditional love. Age is a number, nothing more. We are all on borrowed time, borrowed from an eternity when there is nothing but a void. I believe after this life there is no other, but I believe that certain kinds of love never die. Though the body may be in the ground, the love can still be felt in the gentle breeze that rustles the falling leaves on an autumn morning, in the twinkling of stars in a purple sky at night, in the sun's rays dancing merrily across the horizon at the end of the day, and above all, when the world seems to have placed an unbearable burden upon your shoulders and you sense an invisible hand clutching you, keeping you from falling into the abyss. I have that with my Wayne, and you Jacques have that with Gay. I long for her to awaken from her coma, and if and when she does, do not tarry a day, an hour, a minute until you grasp her with the might of your love and never again let your age difference interfere with your love for one another. You two have waited far too long already to wrap yourselves in the grandeur of your love."

Lynton motioned for Chablis to tell Mr. LaBoche that he might return. As he walked in with Marquet, he went directly to Jacques, who was still seated, placed his right hand on his left shoulder and whispered, "I was wrong, so wrong. I am sorry."

Now, the anger was really building within Marquet. Lynton looked at him with pity, too, because he probably genuinely loved Gay, but was, himself, a victim of circumstance.

LaBoche looked intensely into Jacques eyes and needed no words to convey to him that he harboured no ill feelings for a man who simply loved his daughter. Meanwhile, Chablis, who had always held Lynton in high esteem, was overwhelmed with renewed admiration for this extraordinary woman's kindness and detecting abilities. In fact, she found herself harbouring a bit of jealousy that someone not trained as a detective, as she was, had such an innate observational intellect that made her a force to be reckoned with in the detective business.

Chablis asked Mr. LaBoche if the reporter, Ronald Means, might join them, as he was a man who had enough integrity not to reveal anything that would do harm to the investigation, and that he, having worked diligently on the story, might offer some insightful observations. Having been duly impressed with Chablis and Lynton's astute detecting work, LaBoche saw no reason to deny their request. Thus Bowman went to the car to advise Means that he might join them as they returned to the laboratory.

At some distance from the building, the reporter made all of them stop and, pointing to a small clump of trees to the right said "That's where the intruder came from to get into the bedroom. Am I right?"

Chablis answered him by pointing to the path which ran quite close to the thicket and then to the door of the laboratory. She said, "That path is as you see, topped with gravel, so the man must have passed along it going to the lab, since no traces of his steps have been found on the soft ground. The man didn't have wings; he walked; but he walked on the gravel which left no impression of his tread. The gravel has, in fact, been trodden by many other feet, since the path is the most direct way between the lab and the chateau. As to the thicket, it offered the intruder a sufficient hiding-place until it was time for him to make his way to the lab. It was while hiding in that clump of trees that he saw the opportunity to avail himself of easy entry while Mr. LaBoche and his daughter went for a walk and Jacques was busy in the laboratory.

Chablis and Lynton in the Room of Doom

Gravel has been spread nearly, very nearly, up to the windows of the laboratory. The footprint of a man, parallel with the wall, a mark which we will examine presently, and which I have already seen when we were out here before, prove that he only needed to make one stride to find himself in front of the vestibule window, left open by Jacques. The man drew himself up by his hands and entered the vestibule."

Bowman said, "But how did he get there, in the bushes to start with. Did he just drop out of the sky? There is a gate out front that is the only way in and the back gate is guarded.

"Well, interjected Lynton, "we know now how the man entered by the window, and we also know the moment at which he entered, and obviously hid under the bed until the most propitious time to strike."

Means pointedly asked "But why did he shut the window upon entering? It was an act that might draw the attention of those he was trying to avoid."

Chablis quickly put her index finger to her lips as she looked at Lynton, knowing that she knew the answer. "It may be the window was not shut at once, but if he did shut the window, it was because he was afraid someone might spot him in the vestibule."

Chablis and Lynton in the Room of Doom

All those present but Lynton and Chablis looked puzzled as Bowman said, "What do you mean by that?"

"Not now," replied Chablis. "We'll explain all to you later on when we think the moment to be ripe for doing so as things need a natural progression for definitive answers; but I don't think we have anything of more importance to say on this right now, if my hypothesis is justified."

"And what is your hypothesis," interjected Bowman.

"You will never know if it does not turn out to be the truth. It is of much too grave a nature to speak of it, so long as it continues to be only a hypothesis."

"Have you, at least, some idea as to who the intruder is?"

Again, looking at Lynton, Chablis said, "We do not. But fear not, because with the dynamic dynamo by my side, we shall unravel this mystery."

They all laughed as Lynton shrugged her shoulders and moved to the spot where it was assumed a man had waited patiently for LaBoche and his daughter to leave before he stealthily made his way to where murder was to be attempted.

It was at this time that Bowman made a call to the forensic lab and ordered someone out to make a mould of the footprint they had found.

Chablis, with the others following, went along the wall to the hedge and dry ditch just outside the back gate where Brenner was standing guard now. She leaped over the ditch and said, looking at the small lake in the distance, "This was his nearest way to get out as he made his way to the lake."

Bowman, staring at the lake in the distance, the moonlight glistening off it, said, "How do you know he went to the lake?"

Smiling, she said, "I'm a trained detective."

Lynton, giggling, offered her assessment. "She knows he would not go out the front gate for obvious reasons. The gate in back was unmanned at the time he would have left. Just a calculated guess, but a good one I'd say. As for the lake, well, where else would you head if you did not want to be discovered. Along the road you might, even at that late hour, run into someone coming from the pub after a night of frivolity.

As they were talking, the small party trooped toward the lake. Lake? Well, more like a little sheet of marshy water, surrounded by reeds, on which floated some dead water-lily leaves. A man who may have seen them approaching, but seemed uninterested, as he appeared to be stirring with his cane something which the party of interlopers could not see. Then, suddenly, Bowman, looking down at the ground, said "If these are not the prints of the fellow over there, they may be those of Ms. LaBoche's attacker. They are huge and the man over there is no more than 5"5 or 5:6."

They all looked at them and noticed something else. The footprints came to a halt about 20 feet from the lake and then there were others beside them going in reverse.

"He came down here, and my guess is that man over there was out here that night. The culprit stopped, as you can see the footprints are deeper right there," Lynton said as she pointed down where the footprints came to an abrupt halt. "See, the prints are deeper because he stood there for a second or two, contemplating what he should do, continue on to the lake where he probably had a row boat stashed so he could make it to the other side, or take his chances of being discovered on the road to Cornwall-on-Hudson.

Bowman signalled for the man to come over. He walked to them, and in the better light, Bowman recognized him. "Harry Deter, what are you doing out here so late?"

"I could ask you the same thing Mr. District Attorney, but I know the answer to that."

"Harry," said Bowman respectfully, "Were you here the night of the crime?"

"I was, but I neither heard nor saw anything; otherwise, I would have let you know, obviously. However, now that I give it some thought," Harry said as he pointed over to a small thicket of bushes by the lake, "there was a boat over there that night, a small row boat, but it is gone now, and there was also a bicycle lying in the boat, both not here now."

"It is clearer now," said Chablis as they all walked toward the lakeshore, where she pointed downward at the ground where there were thin bicycle tire marks.

Bowman said, "The man had a bicycle," as he looked at the marks of the bicycle, going and coming? "The bicycle explains the disappearance of the intruder's big footprints. The intruder, with his big boots, mounted a bicycle. His accomplice had come to wait for him on the edge of the lake with the bicycle and row boat. It might be supposed that the intruder was working for the other person, doing his bidding."

"Yes, they might have been in consort," said Lynton showing them the ground where it had been disturbed by big and heavy heels; "the man seated himself there, and took off his hobnailed boots, which he had worn only for the purpose of misleading detection, and then, no doubt, taking them away with him, leaving his accomplice to row back, he stood up in his other boots left here in the bushes, and quietly and slowly regained the road, holding his bicycle in his hand, for he could not venture to ride it and attract the attention of Mr. Deter. That accounts for the lightness of the impression made by the wheels along it, in spite of the softness of the ground. If there had been a man on the bicycle, the wheels would have sunk deeply into the soil. No, no; there was but one man on foot there, the intruder who met with his accomplice."

"Absolutely, my dear comrade," said Chablis as she planted herself in front of LaBoche. "If we had a bicycle here, we might demonstrate the correctness of the young man's reasoning. Do you have one at the chateau?"

"No, there is not." He pointed at Marquet and said, he took it four days ago, to Cornwall, the last time he came to the chateau. He had walked out to the château from town where his car was being serviced and wanted to ride it back. He left it at the Dinwiddie. Obviously, we all forgot about it being there with all the turmoil and upheaval."

Chablis said, "What we need are all the results from the lab. I believe I am beginning to see the light in the darkness in this whole affair, but I need the lab results."

Bowman offered good news. "Tomorrow afternoon, the head of our forensics department is coming to the laboratory at the chateau where he expects to gather all those who have played any part in this tragedy. It will be very interesting I am sure. Obviously, he will have all the lab results."

Lynton, looking at Chablis and winking, said "A night and a morning to kill in Cornwall-on-Hudson, all alone contemplating the nuances of this case." She then turned toward Bowman and smiled. Yeah, she thought. Sure, Chablis will be alone with a good looking man like Bowman interested in her feminine wiles. Chablis was not one to pass up a chance for erotic delight.

CHAPTER 6
LIVE IN YOUR HEART

Take note and examine closely
As the clues unfold one by one
This unidentified assailant mystifies
As Chablis and Lynton, super sleuths
Are the mixtures' vermouths
Picking through with a fine toothed comb
Using their imaginative calculations
One step away from solving this mystery
And as usual they will make history

On the way back to Cornwall-on-Hudson, Bowman was careful to make sure he dropped off Means first, then, as he was going to the hotel to drop off Chablis and Lynton, he asked the girls if they would like a late evening meal. Lynton, knowing that Chablis was anxious for a tête-à-tête with Bowman that would, no doubt, lead to a romantic interlude, begged off, but Chablis accepted. Lynton got out of the car, and said to Chablis as she was closing the door, "I won't wait up for you."

The only non-fast food place open was the Avon Diner which had been around since 1937, and the motif was still retro 1950's, which Chablis found pleasing. They made small talk across the booth, and Bowman was careful to try and not stare at her perky breasts with pointed nipples that seemed to be fighting the tight cotton blouse for freedom.

Chablis and Lynton in the Room of Doom

Chablis knew what Bowman wanted. Hell, she knew what all men wanted, and the odd thing was she wanted it too. She took a deep breath so he could get the full effect of her perky erect extremely dark nipples peeping through her white blouse that fit her taunt body like a glove. She could even sense the rise between his legs. She said, "You seem preoccupied Robert."

"I, I, well Chablis, I don't think I have ever been out with such a beautiful woman."

She leaned over so he could get a nice look at her cleavage. "Well, what a nice thing to say. You know a girl just loves compliments from a man."

"Could I interest you in going back to my place for a drink?"

Smiling provocatively, she replied, "I'd love one."

Bowman kept apologizing for the messiness of his townhouse, but Chablis told him that men just weren't designed to be good housekeepers, and that it was OK. She laughed as she said, "Men are designed for only one thing in their minds, and we both know they think about that 24/7."

He could not resist the opening she offered. "Well, I have to admit that ever since I laid eyes on you that has been on my mind."

Chablis and Lynton in the Room of Doom

Chablis was not coy. "Yes, I noticed your interest Robert, and I am flattered. I assume you are well aware that I am a non-operative transsexual."

"I am."

"And you will not be bothered by what I have between my legs?"

"I am not an idiot Chablis. I know what is between a person's legs does not define gender. I know what a birth defect is."

Laughing, she replied. "Ah, I have heard men describe it many ways, but few are astute enough to realize it is a birth defect. You have been with transsexuals before?"

"No, I have not, and I am afraid you will find me uninterested in one part of your anatomy."

Still smiling, she said, "Well, it does not function well anyway due to hormones, so if it did interest you, you would be very disappointed."

He got up from the chair in which he was sitting and walked over to the sofa and sat beside her. He looked into her eyes as he leaned forward to kiss her succulent, puffy lips. The kiss was like a journey into a paradise of duelling tongues as Chablis melted into his arms.

She threw back her head so his tongue could work its magic in her warm mouth and arched her back and threw back her hair. They came up for air and she reached down between his legs. "Oh my, someone has an erection."

They both laughed and he said, "My bedroom would be more comfortable. "

"I know it would."

They stood by the bed for a few lingering kisses, and then Chablis began to remove her clothes as did Robert. His stiff member stood at attention as she, naked except for her panties, dropped to her knees and devoured his manhood like she had been on a starvation diet and just been offered a banquet of delightful goodies. She sucked every last centremetre into her mouth, gobbling it up and making slurping noises which she knew would make him even more aroused. How she loved the power her mouth exercised over men. It was not the sex act itself that thrilled her, but the sense of power it gave her. Men were putty in her hands once she had their member in her mouth. "Damn, I am good," she thought to herself. "No, I am the damn best."

She stood up and very adroitly lowered her panties, being careful to keep her member stuck between her legs, making it invisible. All Robert noticed was glorious flesh and, unlike most women who had been brainwashed into shaving their pubic hair, hers was massive, thick and reached almost to her navel. She backed herself just slightly out of reach and asked him if he wanted to touch her mass of pubic hair. Almost pleading he said, "Please, please."

She reached up to his broad shoulders and forced him onto his knees. "Go ahead and nestle in it. Feel its warmth, smell its sensual odour and kiss it."

Robert kissed, smelled and nestled in its warmth for several minutes as she lightly rubbed his shoulders, making sure she kept her legs together. She finally reached down and pulled him up to her. As they kissed, she pulled him onto the bed on top of her. He was a big man, maybe 6:2, and had just a bit of a belly on him, as most men in their late 40's do. He worked his way down to her breasts and suckled like a baby who was starved for the nourishment they offered.

"I want your cock inside me," she whispered as she pushed him off to her left, then turned over on her stomach, exposing the most fantastic ass upon which Robert had ever gazed. It was not just an ass. It was a work of art, as the cheeks were perfectly symmetrical and the softness of the flesh called Robert to rest his face upon it, to feel the softness and to delight in the serenity the flesh offered him. He lingered there in this heaven.

Chablis and Lynton in the Room of Doom

Chablis, needing to have her aching cavity filled with Robert's manhood, began to wiggle and squirm.

Spread thy closed curtain of delight,
Sex-performing cheeks of love's night.
That runaway eyes may gladly wink.
Leap my stiff member into the breech,
So that she may suck you in like a leech.
Plunge deep into the dark hole that waits.
Lovers in ecstasy do their amorous rites.
Those two cheeks spread for great delights.
By Chablis' own designs, she squeezes.
Cum, cum, cum and ram, ram and ram,
Plunge deep within like a sacrificial lamb.
Those soft cushions flatten to the shove.
And long with passion your seed to win.
How could something this good be a sin?
Play them the game of lover's in heat.
"Ram me baby, ram me hard with might.
And I shall melt in love's grand delight."

After an intense explosion into her gapping anal cavity, Robert rolled off her and lay exhausted on the field of love where the battle of fantastic fornication had delightfully spent all his energy in the ecstasy of lovemaking. He lay there for maybe thirty minutes basking in the glorious afterglow of the finest moment of sexual blissfulness that he had ever experienced in his 47 years. Chablis lay in his arms, wrapping herself in his warmth. She was made for the act of love.

Chablis and Lynton in the Room of Doom

He said to her softly, "Chablis, I have never experienced anything like that before. Wow, I am overwhelmed."

She provocatively whispered, "You aren't through yet sweetheart," as she worked her way down between his legs and began the rhythmic arousal of that organ that she longed for more of in that dark place deep inside her that craved satisfaction that she could only get from a man's stiff member. She let it pop out of her mouth for a second or two and said, as if talking to it rather than him, "Ah, this is my big lollipop. This is my toy, and I am like a kid who will not stop playing. Oh baby, how my little brown hole craves your stiffness inside me."

She moved her mouth up and down the shaft, slick with spit. He pushed upward into her warm mouth and she made way in her throat for him, as far back as he could thrust. He could hear the juiciness of her mouth and was filled with delight when he hit the back of her throat. "Umm" she muttered, never once gagging as she had conditioned herself to take the biggest of the big.

She crawled up on him, sitting on his face, offering him her hole to lick. He began to tongue her deep as she rode his darting dancer of demented delicious delight as if she was a trained equestrian riding a horse across the green pasture of pleasure.

She, not asking but demanding, said, "Make it wet for us baby." She wriggled, putting his hot mouth and tongue where she wanted it. He entered her with his tongue, pushing deeper and deeper. Then, she quickly moved away, placing her bare bodacious beautiful ass on his stiff member that was standing like a flagpole. She reached back and spread her cheeks, then she lowered herself onto him, just enough to squeeze in the tip of his throbbing member. She held it there, bouncing so slightly, the inner muscles clenching, then pulled out. She was teasing him unmercifully. "If you want it baby come and get it. Get it hard and furious."

He pushed his body up with his hands, trying to get some leverage, trying to ram her hole with his massive erection. She shouted, "You have to try harder than that! What, do you have two broken legs? Come on baby. Come on and ram me, ram me."

Robert was like a man dying in the desert and there was an oasis in the distance just waiting with a babbling brook where he could satisfy his voracious thirst. He never wanted anything so much in his life. He pulled her down onto him hard. He strained upward, thrusting with all his force. She kept her butt spread wide open and was toying with him by occasionally squeezing his love muscle with her skilled contractions "Don't you want it?" she mockingly kept asking him.

"Yes, yes," he shouted.

He reached for her gorgeous perfectly rounded symmetrical breasts and massaged them. He twisted her dark gumdrop nipples and made her groan. With that she sat down on his member until it was snug deep within her. "Ah!" she cried out. She jiggled and bounced on top of him, the perfect meat of her haunches reverberating with sweaty delight. He grabbed her by the shoulders, bringing her eager hole down and down again onto his stiffness.

She pulled his hands over her own hands and onto her breasts. Together they kneaded and squeezed, twisted her nipples so hard that she squirmed. She said, "Tell me, have you been thinking of this ever since you first laid eyes on me, saw my wantonness and knew you had to have my ass?"

As he continued to thrust, thrust, thrust like he was a piston in a race car engine at the speedway he shouted, "Yes, yes, I dreamed of fucking you, dreamed of this very moment when I would be getting the ride of my life."

She let him maul her breasts. She made him feel as if she were his sex machine, something warm and durable that existed only for his pleasure and excitement. She rode him harder and harder. He said, "I want to make you cum, if I can."

Chablis and Lynton in the Room of Doom

"Just keep it up baby. Keep it up and it will happen," she shouted as she put her hands around her member and began to pump. He began to slap at her gorgeous ass, the sound echoing off the bedroom walls. Her strong muscular thighs kept her hovered above, feeding his erection into her hole. Her right hand worked quickly back and forth on her now stiffened member, her moans getting louder. "Now, here it comes." she shouted. Her cheeks flushed and her muscles tightened as she shuddered in orgasmic delight pulsating violently with the white gooey joy juice squirting all over Robert's chest. Then, Robert exploded like a volcano deep inside her cavity. He let out a long, slow moan and collapsed in ecstasy.

She crawled off him and said, "I'll have your seed inside me all night. It will do until in the morning, when you will mount this mare like a stallion and do it all over again."

The next morning, Chablis and Robert showed up looking exhausted. Lynton, smiling, said, "You two look tired."

Chablis winked at her and said, "He is not a DA. He is an A.D."

Lynton did not ask what she meant by that term, but Chablis bent over and whispered to Robert. "A.D. that means in my lingo, ass driver, and boy did you drive mine last night."

Chablis and Lynton in the Room of Doom

Back to Bowman's home again they went, as Chablis said she needed to look at the estate for there was something she was missing. She felt that they were all being too logical in their approach. There was something illogical about the whole affair.

Lynton said, "This morning, we examined the handkerchief. I am beginning to think that the numberless little round scarlet stains, the impression of drops in the tracks of the footprints, at the moment when they were made on the floor, prove to me that the intruder was not wounded at all. The blood was splattered about like the kind of bleed you get from the nose. The man could have allowed the blood to flow into his hand and handkerchief, and dried his hand on the wall. As detectives, we can often twist logic to the necessities of preconceived ideas. We have in our minds a theory that demands the intruder should have been wounded in the hand, otherwise it comes to nothing."

Chablis said, "You are right. We are missing the obvious, but what is the obvious?"

They were greeted by the maid who ushered them into the parlour and said, "Mr. LaBoche will be down momentarily."

Chablis, looking at Robert, offered an observation. "This place is very sterile looking."

"What do you mean," replied Robert.

"It is as if there is no life here, as if there is something missing."

"Yes, I agree," interjected Lynton. "It is almost antiseptic. There is no happiness here, but my guess is that it is something that has been enhanced in misery by the situation with Gay LaBoche." Then, she completely changed the subject. "Did you notice that when the revelation about Gay and Jacques was exposed, Marquet, although perturbed, did not manifest intense anger? My guess is he knew about their affair."

"True," offered Chablis. "I would surmise as you that he must have known."

LaBoche walked in with a forlorn look on his face. He looked at the three and said, "I have to decide soon. I cannot let her continue to suffer." He sat down, no, flopped down in a chair by the fireplace.

Chablis said, "It is understandable that you are agonizing, and I know it is a tough decision. We will try to stay out of your way as much as possible and not bother you. Just a couple of questions and we will be out of your hair."

"I am sorry. I know you are doing all you can to solve this mystery. I shall help all I can."

"We need to know about the proprietors of the Dinwiddie," said Chablis as she walked over to the fireplace and stood in front of it. "What kind of people are they. Your sincere and honest appraisal, please."

"A little eccentric, like me I suppose. They were friendly toward me, as I would drop by for a brandy on occasion as I walked from the train station on after going into Manhattan on business. Nothing that unusual about them. Both in their late 40's. I would say that Ms. Lorton was definitely the smarter one, and was obviously the one who was, as it is said in today's vernacular, the top in their relationship. She appears a bit bossy in regards to her husband at times – no, most of the time. They actually bought the inn at almost the exact time I bought this place, just a few weeks afterward."

"In regards to your decision to encourage your daughter not to get involved with Jacques," said Lynton in an almost whisper, "was that a point of contentiousness between the two of you?"

"You mean my daughter and me?"

"Yes."

"It was, and until this day, until I realized yesterday when so much was brought out here in this very room, it was a barrier to happiness."

"But you also knew, did you not, of their clandestine meetings, as you assumed the shadow you often saw in the dim lit room was his," asked Chablis.

"I did, and much to my shame, I was furious that she was in love with someone I thought beneath her station in life. I am not like that believe me. I suppose it was just that I loved her so much that I wanted the best for her, but now I realize that Jacques was the best, because he adores her, and he might not be as intelligent as she, nor as successful, and he is much older but his love is genuine and pure. I was a fool."

Lynton said, "Do not be too hard on yourself. It is natural for a father to want the best for his daughter, but sometimes we lose sight of their need to make their own decisions, even if it might be the wrong decisions. Life is like your lab experiments. Sometimes we mix the wrong chemicals and an explosion can occur, but other times we get just the right combination of elements and everything turns out perfect. Life, itself, is an experiment."

He looked up at her and said, "You are a wise woman."

Giggling, she replied, "I am sure my boyfriend Wayne might take issue with that assessment." Then, they all laughed.

J. Wayne Frye

Chablis and Lynton in the Room of Doom

The Dinwiddie Inn was of no imposing appearance; it was two centuries old according to the date marker. Under its sign-board just as you entered, right by the threshold, a man with a crabbed-looking face was standing, seemingly plunged in unpleasant thought, if the wrinkles on his forehead and the knitting of his brows were any indication. He asked, in a tone anything but engaging, whether they wanted anything. He was, no doubt, the not very amiable Mr. Lorton.

"I am the District Attorney," said Robert.

"Big fucking deal," replied Lorton. "I ain't done nothing wrong, so I ain't scarping and bowing to you." Then, he looked at Chablis and continued. "You were in here the other night. Nice little morsel you are. Yes, nice indeed." He then turned to Lynton and said, "Now, you are a little bit of brown delight girl. I bet you are a Filipino."

Lynton did not speak, just nodded her head yes. The gas fireplace was turned on and the place was actually too warm as Robert asked if they might have a word with him and his wife.

"I don't have to talk to you unless you got a warrant. I don't cotton to coppers much. You guys got a damn bad habit of shooting first and asking questions later. Every week some damn poor slob gets blown away by you fucking Nazi storm troopers."

Chablis and Lynton in the Room of Doom

Suddenly, Lynton said to Lorton, "The presbytery has lost nothing of its charm, nor the garden its brightness."

Lorton immediately put his right index finger to his lips, which evidently signified that he had not only determined not to speak, but also enjoined silence on all there. Suddenly, as Lorton motioned for them to take a seat, an intense scowl of hatred manifested itself on his face.

His face was expressing fierce hatred. He went and glued himself to one of the windows, watching the road. Chablis, Lynton and Robert went to the other window right beside the one he was gazing out to see what was attracting Lorton's attention. A man who was dressed entirely in green velvet, his head covered with a huntsman's cap of the same colour, advanced leisurely down the side of the road, lighting a pipe as he walked.. He carried a big leather bag slung over his right shoulder. This man was obviously the reason for Mr. Lorton's intense concern.

The man's movements displayed an almost aristocratic bearing. He wore eye-glasses and appeared to be around fifty years old. His hair was immaculately combed and he had a neatly trimmed salt and pepper moustache, mostly salt. He was remarkably handsome thought both Chablis and Lynton. As he passed near the inn, he hesitated, as if asking himself whether or not he should enter it; gave a glance towards the window where the four stood, took a few whiffs at his pipe, and then resumed his walk away from the pub at the same nonchalant pace.

The three investigators looked at Lorton. His flashing eyes, his clenched hands, his trembling lips, told of the intensely agitated feelings. Lorton, very pointedly said, "He did damn well for himself by not coming in here today."

"Who is he?" asked Chablis.

"That my curious trio is the green man, Joe Lowman."

"I don't know him," said Bowman.

"Then all the better for you. He is not an acquaintance to make. He happens to be Mr. LaBoche's gardener. I am surprised you have not met him since you have all been nosing around out there on a wild goose chase. Nobody likes that asshole. He is an arrogant, bombastic know-it-all, whom I believe comes from money just by his bearing, but obviously, he must have lost it all if he is but a gardener at the LaBoche chateau."

"He acts all high and mighty, but a gardener is as much a servant as any other, isn't he? Upon my word, he would say that he is the master of the grounds of the estate rather than admit to being just an ordinary gardener. He'll not let a poor creature eat a morsel of bread on the grass. Pardon me, on his grass!"

"Does he come here often?" asked Chablis.

"Too often. But I've made him understand that he isn't welcome here. He has a room off Maine Street, stays at Lynette Richelieu's boarding house. Mr. High and Mighty can't even afford to rent an apartment. That suits him fine though, as he probably is not paying any rent, as he is courting Ms. Richelieu. She is a rich widow and totally bonkers, so he picks 'um well."

Bowman said, "He has a reputation for being a bad fellow, then?"

"There isn't a decent man who can stand him. Why, the other workers at the chateau wouldn't offer him a drink of water if he was dying of thirst."

Chablis, as they all walked away from the window and had a seat, said, while Lorton's wife came over to asked what they wanted to drink, "We are here to ask what you think of the break-in and assault of Ms. LaBoche. You said you heard shots and a cat."

"Ms. LaBoche," he said as his wife sat down the drinks at the table.

"Yes," said Bowman. "We want to know your opinion."

"She was a nice girl, very nice and polite. She didn't put on airs at all, despite being rich and famous."

Mrs. Lorton dressed in what one would probably describe as rags, pulled up a seat, her greying hair hanging loosely over her wrinkled forehead, and said, "We don't want to get involved in this whole affair. We just told what we saw. That's it."

Suddenly, a cat came up to the table and meowed as it scurried slowly about Mrs. Lorton's feet, apparently filled with affection for her. She just ignored it. While this was going on, Lynton saw it as an opportunity to bring up the cry of the cat on the night of the assault. "You seem to have a fine furry friend there."

"My cat yes. She is only friendly toward me."

Lynton continued. "The night of the assault, you and your husband heard the cry of a cat, despite it being so far away?"

"You calling us liars? We heard shots and a cat howling, yes."

"No, not calling you liars at all —seems strange to hear those sounds all the way down here."

"Well, we heard 'um," she indignantly replied.

Then, an old, very old and sad looking woman walked in with a huge cat, a Maine Coon Cat, trailing along by her side. The cat at Mrs. Lorton's feet scurried away in fright from the much larger, more sinister looking cat. The cat began a slow, methodical cry that seemed to rock the walls. As if drawn by the cat's cry a man followed the old woman in. It was the green man. He saluted by raising his hand to his cap and seated himself at a table nearby. The green man looked over at the party at the table, and eyeing Mrs. Lorton bellowed, "A lager of beer – Guinness, of course."

Lorton barked, "Ain't got nothing here to serve you. Kindly leave."

"This is a public house of intoxicants. Asked the D.A. sitting there beside you and his two fancy lady friends from Manila and New York if you don't have to serve me as long as I am not causing a disturbance."

"Serve him," said Robert.

The Green Man was obviously very knowledgeable about the three guests. He eased back in his chair and said, "Mr. D.A., you might sully your stellar reputation hanging out with a man who poses as a lady. I'd be more careful about who I chose to have drinks with."

Chablis and Lynton in the Room of Doom

You could tell immediately that Robert was ready to make a charge at him and deliver some furious blows for the offence aimed at Chablis, but before he could get up, Chablis, who had endured many such malcontents over the years, placed her hand on Robert's arm to restrain him. She looked directly into Lowman's eyes and said, "Listen here you bombastic cretin, I am more woman than a low-life, arrogant asshole like you could ever handle." Then she looked at his companion and continued her diatribe. "That woman may put up with you because she can do no better than an asshole like you. Me, I have too much respect for myself to curry favour from a jack-ass who probably can't get an erection, and if you could, you wouldn't know how to use it. You fuck with me, and I'll shove my high heel up your ass. No, no I want, because a homophobic fuck like you would probably enjoy it. You are the kind of guy who secretly dreams of having a cock up your ass. I have dealt with men, no, with sorry excuses of men, like you all my life. Right now you are fantasizing about me, dreaming of what it would be like to get hold of a real woman for a change, not the pathetic dowagers who cater to your arrogance."

He started to get up, but as he did, so did Lynton, and she stood there with her beautiful brown defiant body right beside Chablis and said, "Get up jerk and you'll taste the heels from hell. Believe me, you won't feel like a man when I am through grinding my heels into your groin."

Robert was smiling from ear to ear. He had never seen two such magnificent women in all his life. He eased back in his chair, looked over at Lowman and said, "Messed with the wrong women this time."

Lowman got up and stormed out, but his companion, the lady of late night mausoleum journey fame, Ms. Richelieu, simply sat there dumbfounded with her huge cat by her feet. She looked over at the three and said, "There are no two cats in the world that cry the same. Well, on the night of the assault I also heard the cry of the banshee's cat behind the chateau and it scared my cat. I swear. I crossed myself when I heard that, as if I had heard the devil. There was real evil about that night."

Chablis, seeing an opening to question the lady cited as being crazy, said, "So, you were behind the chateau that night going to the cemetery."

"I go 2 or 3 nights a week, visit my daughter's mausoleum late night, because she likes it that way. She talks better late at night. We sometimes talk into the wee hours of the morning."

"I see," said Chablis as she got up, went over and had a seat at Ms. Richelieu's table and reached down to stroke the cat.

Chablis and Lynton in the Room of Doom

"Her name is Kitten. She is 7 years old. Big cats don't live long you know."

"Yes, I had a wonderful cat when I was a little girl. Used to walk to school with me every morning, and then would be waiting for me at the end of the day. He was such a loyal cat."

"Yes, they are much better than dogs, much better. You are from New York City aren't you? You and your friend over there are very beautiful ladies."

"Well, thank you so much. All we women love compliments, even when it comes from another woman."

Lynton and Robert watched Chablis work her magic with admiration. She was laying the foundation for getting the woman to trust her and open up with information about the case.

Chablis had established rapport now, and began to hone in on what she needed to learn. "I am Chablis Louise Chavez. I am a private investigator working on the LaBoche assault case. You are familiar with it obviously."

"Of course."

"You were out walking behind the château that night?"

"I was, yes. I was visiting my daughter, going to have a nice long chat with her."

"How nice. And you heard a wailing cat?"

"Yes, yes. Oh my, it was not a good cat. No, it was definitely a black cat of evil."

"That is all you heard. You did not hear anything else?"

"I heard two gunshots, just after hearing the cat's horrible moaning."

"The gunshots came immediately after the cat howling?"

"Yes, immediately after."

"Is there anything else you could add that might help us in finding the intruder?"

"No, I was scared, so I hurried to the cemetery. Didn't want my daughter to worry about me."

"That's nice. You are a good mom."

"Can you help me? Help me find my daughter's killer. She talks to me, but she is dead you know."

"Nobody is dead as long as they live in your heart, Ms. Richelieu."

CHAPTER 7
THERE IN LIES THE RUB

Memory of the assault is a flickering flame
Gay was this woman's grand name
It's strange how things come to an end
How thoughts go flashing back again
To kindle, yes kindle that flame

Dear Gay had such fascinating ways
A deep dark gaze in her sultry eyes
She had a lover Jacques in crimson skies
Oh, how passionate their attempts at love
But others made mischief thereof

It is now but a slowly smouldering flame
My oh my Gay is such a sweet name
But things would never be the same
Until there was discovery of what became
Of Gay in the room of doom's hot flame

Jacques fired up that flickering flame
This girl with the sweet sounding name
Merriment was her name way back then
Now thoughts go flashing back again
To the day someone tried to smother the flame

Can you feel the heat from the flame
Jacques and Gay together were never tame
Until someone put hands around neck
And it was then that a dark cloud came
And nothing would ever be the same.

Chablis and Lynton in the Room of Doom

Someone was bordering on the insane
Playing a most deadly game
What could it mean this dastardly act
On that girl with the sweet sounding name
When someone wanted to douse the flame

Into the breech came women of distinction
Who would make a brilliant prediction
They never met a foe they could not tame
Chablis and Lynton were the culprit's affliction
And again there would be heat from the flame

Over the years, the mystery of the room of doom has grown into a mild legend among mystery aficionados. Among the mass of papers, legal documents, memoirs, and extracts from newspapers, which this writer has collected over the years there is one interesting piece that stands out above all the others. It is the detail of what is one of the most tantalizing, astute, mesmerizing examinations by a detective in the annals of detecting. The following narrative comes directly from Lynton Viñas, who secretly recorded the entire examination and then transcribed it by hand in order to add comments. She took the original recording, rerecorded it from her cell phone onto a cassette and placed it in a vault for posterity. Then she simply handed me the transcript she had made, shaking her head and saying, "Remarkable, and you are a writer. Do with it as you will. It is amazing. Chablis is a genius." So, after all these years, I now share it with you.

Chablis and Lynton in the Room of Doom

The assemblage of the principals took place in the laboratory. All present were about to be mesmerized by Chablis perceptive examination and presentation of the facts, which were merely intended to rouse the culprit, not solve the crime. What follows is the manuscript as given to me.

The examining magistrate, Chablis and I (Lynton) found ourselves in the place we had called the Room of Doom in the company of the builder who had constructed the laboratory according to LaBoche's desires. He had a workman with him who had laid the walls entirely bare; that is to say, he had them stripped of the paper which had decorated them. Blows with a pick, here and there, satisfied us of the absence of any sort of opening. The floor and the ceiling were thoroughly sounded. We found nothing. There was nothing to be found. Robert kept saying, "What a case! What a case! We shall never know how the intruder was able to get out of this room!"

After discussions with the two men, Chablis nodded to Robert, who said to one of the uniformed officers with him, "Go to the chateau and request LaBoche, Marquet and Jacques to come here please. Also, ask the Brenner's to come. One of you can watch the back gate for Mr. Brenner. Also, one of you please wait at the front, as I have summoned the Lorton's here, too." He then turned to Chablis and said, "It is all yours Chablis. You are in charge from here on.

Five minutes later all were assembled in the laboratory. Chablis said, "With your permission, we shall abandon the old system of interrogation. I will not have you brought before me one by one, but we will all remain here as we are. We are on the spot where the crime was committed. We have nothing else to discuss but the crime. So let us discuss it freely, intelligently or otherwise, so long as we speak just what is in our minds. There need be no formality or method since this won't help us in any way."

Then, passing among the gathering, she looked at LaBoche and said, "You have been seriously aggrieved, as your daughter was everything to you, and we are here to see if we can somehow lay bare the cold hard facts, which will not restore your daughter to health, but will let you know the details of what occurred. The why will fall into place eventually, but to get there we must somehow figure out how the culprit got out of the room. This is, without a doubt, the most baffling case I have ever confronted.

There was strangeness about LaBoche. His clear, soft, blue eyes expressed infinite sorrow. He was a man who devoted his life to science, but in reality, his life was really his daughter, and she appeared to be beyond hope, as her imminent death was almost assured once he made the faithful decision to pull the plug, which would have to come soon.

Chablis and Lynton in the Room of Doom

His daughter was always to be seen either following him or by his side; for they never quitted each other, it was said, and had shared the same labours most of their lives The young lady had devoted herself entirely to science. She still won admiration for her imperial beauty which had remained intact, without a wrinkle, withstanding time and love. Who would have dreamed that Chablis should one day be in the room where Gay was put almost to the point of death, painfully recounting to those present the most monstrous and most mysterious crimes in the annals of mysteries? Who would have thought that she should be, that afternoon, listening to the despairing father vainly trying to explain how his daughter's assailant had been able to escape from him? They had buried themselves with their work in obscurity only to meet with calamity.

Chablis walked over to LaBoche and said, "Now, place yourself exactly where you were when Gay left you to go to her bedroom."

LaBoche rose, and standing at a certain distance from the door of the room of doom, said, in an even voice and without the least trace of emphasis, "I was here, after I had made a brief chemical experiment at the beakers of the laboratory, needing all the space behind me, I had my desk moved here by Jacques, who spent the evening in cleaning some of my apparatus. My daughter had been working at the same desk with me. When it was her time to leave she rose, kissed me, and bade Jacques goodnight. She had to pass behind my desk and the door to enter her bedroom, and she could do this only with some difficulty. That is to say, I was very near the place where the crime occurred later."

"And the desk?" asked Chablis. "Right after the disturbance and criers from her room what became of it?"

"I am not sure what you mean."

Jacques interrupted. "We pushed it back against the wall, here—close to where it is at the present moment, so as to be able to get at the door at once."

"So, the desk was right by the door, a little to the right, but almost in front of it? Might not a man in the room, in the confusion when you got in have somehow made it to the desk, it being so near to the door, by stooping and slipping under the desk, and then left unobserved?"

"No, absolutely not as my daughter had locked and bolted her door, the door had remained fastened, then we vainly tried to force it open when we heard the noise, and then we were at the door while the struggle between the intruder and my poor child was going on. Immediately after we heard her stifled cries as she was being held by the fingers that had left their red mark upon her throat. Rapid as the attack was, we were no less rapid in our endeavours to get into the room where the tragedy was taking place."

Chablis walked to the door rose once more and examined it with the greatest care. Then she returned to her original place with a despairing gesture. "If the lower panel of the door could be removed without the whole door being necessarily opened, the problem would be solved. But, unfortunately, that last hypothesis is untenable after an examination of the door as it's of oak, solid and massive. You can see that quite plainly, in spite of the damage done in the attempt to burst it open."

Chablis had no sooner uttered these words when the Lorton's walked in, and with a motion pointing at two chairs, Chablis indicated they should be seated. Turning to the Brenner's she said to them, "tell us what you were doing at the time Ms. LaBoche was being attacked; for you were close to the lab Mr. Brenner and obviously, Mrs. Brenner was not far away."

"We had both heard the commotion, and we were preparing to help," replied Mr. Brenner.

"And what of the firing of the pistol?" coyly said the shrewd Chablis, wording it in a way to catch them in a lie.

"Yes, we heard a shot, both of us. My wife looked out the side window of the cottage at me sitting by the gate when we heard it."

"Heard it? Say again, please?"

Mrs. Brenner said, "When we heard the shot."

"There were two shots, but you heard one?"

"Two shots were fired," said Jacques. "I am certain that all the cartridges were in my revolver. We found afterward that two had been exploded, and we heard two shots behind the door. Was not that so, Mr. LaBoche?"

"Yes, absolutely, two shots – one dull almost muffled and the other ringing, kind of vibrating, sort of echoing." replied LaBoche.

Chablis, moving in front of the Brenner's, stared intently at them. "Why do you persist in lying? Do you think the police are the fools you are? Everything points to the fact that both of you were out of doors and near the lab at the time of the tragedy. What were you doing there? So far as I am concerned I can only explain the escape of the intruder on the assumption of help from these two right here."

They both sat up straighter and looked worried as Mr. Brenner said. "No, no!"

J. Wayne Frye

Chablis and Lynton in the Room of Doom

"You both entered the vestibule did you not?"

Mr. Brenner replied, "Yes."

While there was mass confusion after the door was finally opened, everyone was occupied with Ms. LaBoche. Mr. LaBoche and Jacques both adored Gay and were frantic, not thinking clearly and were confused. You two could have easily facilitated the flight of the intruder, who, screening himself behind you, reached the window in the vestibule, and sprang out of it into the yard. Mr. or Mrs. Brenner closed the window after him and fastened the blinds, which certainly could not have closed and fastened themselves. That is the conclusion I have arrived at. If anyone here has any other idea," and then she turned toward Lynton as she concluded, "let him or her state it."

Lynton said, "What you say was impossible. I do not believe either in the guilt or in the connivance of these two. I say it was impossible, because Mrs. Brenner held fast by the door and did not move from the threshold of the room; because Mr. LaBoche, as soon as the door was forced open, threw himself on his knees beside his daughter, and no one could have left or entered the room by the door, without passing over her body! Mr. Jacques had but to cast a glance around the bedroom and under the bed to see that there was nobody in the room but Gay LaBoche lying on the floor comatose."

Chablis and Lynton in the Room of Doom

"The real key here," said Chablis as she meandered about the room, "is finding a motive for the crime. A motive might help in explaining how the culprit got out of the room." She then stopped in front of Marquet, looked at him intently for awhile, before saying, "OK, the truth. You knew about the affair between Gay and Daniel Jacques. Right?

"No. The first I knew of it was when it was revealed back at the chateau. I'm still in shock. He is not worthy of her."

"Oh, really, because he is just a servant and you are a Ph.D. with a record of what you think are great achievements?"

"I am successful, yes. I am not ashamed of that. I worked hard to get my degrees while he was scrubbing floors."

Chablis walked over to Jacques. If there was one thing that drove both she and Lynton crazy it was arrogance. Standing by Jacques, who lowered his head, she said, "Everybody has value you arrogant, pompous ass. The surgeon may perform the operation, but somebody needs to clean the operating room afterward. So, the janitor has value, too. Jacques' value cannot be measured by the degrees he does or does not hold, but by the devotion and dedication he has shown the LaBoche's over the years."

Chablis and Lynton in the Room of Doom

Robert smiled as Marquet was seething with anger toward Chablis. He got up and started for her, but she said, "Better think twice asshole. I am not the kind of girl you want to mess with. Go ahead, try it. You'll spend the rest of the night trying to pick what's left of your balls off the floor."

Marquet stopped in his tracks, stood there, breathing heavily and slowly sat back down as Chablis said, "I did that just to see whether you had a temper or not. You do! My guess is if you knew about the affair, you would have been capable of a fit of rage and maybe have attacked Gay."

He said nothing, just set there seething with rage. Chablis began her stroll about the room again. Looking at Marquet, she said, "So, you were all set to marry."

"Yes, I hoped we would marry."

"Hope," questioned Chablis. You hoped. Sounds as if you had your doubts. You expressed a hope; but the hope implies a doubt. Why do you doubt?"

"He doubts," interjected LaBoche, "because he was never sure she would have left me. And you know what; now that I really know him, and have seen the value of Jacques and his devotion I am genuinely pleased he will not be my son-in-law."

Chablis and Lynton in the Room of Doom

A dead silence followed LaBoche's words. It was a moment fraught with suspense. Chablis said, "One of the motives for the crime was actually theft. All of you come with me into the hallway, please."

She led them to the lavatory and pointed to a spot on the tile floor. "The stones of the lavatory have not been washed for some time," she said, "that can be seen by the layer of dust that covers them. Now, notice here, the very faint marks of two large footprints and the minute traces of very black dirt they left where they have been. That dirt comes from but one place, as most of the ground around here is clay. There is one spot down by the lake where the dirt is very black and moist in the mornings. What the intruder did was to come here before 10:00 AM, when there was nobody around, and attempted his robbery."

Chablis walked to a place beside the front door, and pointed down at the floor. "See, can you see that small fibre there, imbedded in the baseboard. I did not remove it, but I know what it is. It is burlap."

"Burlap?" interjected Robert.

"Yes, burlap from a large bag the intruder had with him, a burlap bag. He placed it down here for a brief time by the wall, and when he did part of the burlap caught on the baseboard."

"When I saw the mark of the parcel by the side here, I had no doubt as to the robbery. The thief had not brought a parcel with him; he had picked it up here. Mr. LaBoche, you have burlap bags in the laboratory as they are used to delivery items you use in your experiments. Right?"

"Yes."

"He had also placed his heavy boots beside the parcel, which is why there are no marks of steps leading to the marks left by the boots, which were placed side by side. That accounts for the fact that the intruder left no trace of his steps when he fled from the bedroom, nor any in the laboratory, nor in the vestibule. After entering the bedroom in his boots, he took them off, finding them troublesome, or because he wished to make as little noise as possible. The marks made by him in going through the vestibule and the laboratory were subsequently washed out later in the day by Mr. Jacques, right? You did clean here that morning. Am I correct?"

"Yes, yes, I did," replied Jacques.

"Having, for some reason or other, taken off his boots, the intruder carried them in his hand and placed them by the side of the parcel he had picked up in the lab as by that time the robbery had been accomplished. The man then returned to bedroom and slipped under the bed, where the mark of his body is perfectly visible on the floor and even on the mat, which has been slightly moved from its place and creased. Fragments of straw also, recently torn, bear witness to the intruder's movements under the bed."

"But we looked under the bed," said a surprised Jacques.

"Yes, I know, but he was gone from there by then. I will get to that shortly."

"But why did he not just leave when he had the chance," asked Robert.

"And what did he steal? said LaBoche.

"All in good time my friends. Be patient. The robber had another motive for returning to hide under the bed," continued the astonishing Chablis. "You might think that he was trying to hide himself quickly on seeing, through the vestibule window, the people about to enter the building. It would have been much easier for him to have climbed up to the attic and hidden there, waiting for an opportunity to get away, if his purpose had been only flight, but no, he had to be in that bedroom."

Robert said, "That's all possible I suppose. However, we need to know what he stole and why. There is nothing missing."

"Something very valuable," replied Chablis as she pointed to the lab and bade they all follow her as she walked over to a cabinet and pointed Mr. LaBoche toward it as she said, "You rarely have need to open this, right?"

Dumbfounded, as he stood in front of it, he said, "No, no it is my notes from years of work."

Chablis pulled it open and the top shelf was empty. LaBoche nearly collapsed and had to be helped to a chair by Jacques. As he sat down, almost in tears, trembling, he said, "I have been robbed again! My notes from my life's work are gone, and I never put any of it on a computer disc, stupid, so stupid. The details of secret experiments and our labours were in that cabinet. It is an irreparable loss to us and, I venture to say, to science. All the processes by which I had been able to arrive at the precious proof of the destructibility of matter were there, all. The man who came wished to take all from me, my daughter and my work, my heart and my soul."

And, head in hands, the strain of the past few days was just too much for him. He wept like a baby as all there were silent, deeply affected by the great man's grief.

Chablis turned to the cabinet and, pointing at the empty top shelf, broke the almost solemn silence. She entered into explanations, for which there was great need, as to why she had been led to believe that a robbery had been committed, which included the simultaneous discovery she had made in the lavatory, and the empty top shelf in the cabinet. The first thing that had struck her, she said, was the unusual form of that piece of furniture. It was very strongly built of fire-proof iron, clearly showing that it was intended for the keeping of most valuable objects. Then she noticed that the key had been left in the lock. 'One does not ordinarily have a safe and leave the key in it!' she said to herself. This little key, with its brass head had strongly attracted me; its presence suggested robbery." She turned toward LaBoche and said, "Who usually keeps that key?"

"Why Gay. She was never without it."

Lynton had been exceedingly quiet all this time, but Chablis turned to her and gave her that look – the look that said, "Go ahead and put in your two cents worth."

Nodding her head in acknowledgement, Lynton said, "If that key never left Gay's person, the intruder must have waited for her in her room for the purpose of stealing it; and the robbery could not have been committed until after the attack had been made on her. But after the attack four persons were in the laboratory." She looked back at Chablis and shrugged her shoulders, indicating she was confused.

J. Wayne Frye

Chablis and Lynton in the Room of Doom

Smiling, Chablis reached into her blouse pocket and pulled out a paper she had copied when in the library. It was from the local newspaper, a classified ad, dated the day before the attack. She read from it. "Cornwall-on-Hudson Herald: Yesterday a black satin small ladies purse was lost. It contained, amongst other things, a small key with a brass head. A handsome reward will be given to the person returning it. Please contact gbincharge@yahoo.com. Is that your daughter's e-mail, Mr. LaBoche?

"It is."

"The key thus winds up," said Chablis as she pointed at it in the lock, "here." Sorry Lynton that I did not discuss it with you. I did not think it important at the time, which is why I put it in my blouse pocket and forgot it. I was getting ready to wash it last night and found it there and just put two and two together."

Lynton nodded her head, and Robert said, "I'll have to remember to always check the classifieds on line and in the paper in future cases. Brilliant work that we would have probably never been discovered by us. I will get a subpoena to assess replying e-mail account as yahoo requires a cell phone for confirmation to establish an account."

"No need, he probably used a throw away phone to get the e-mail account," offered Lynton.

Chablis and Lynton in the Room of Doom

Chablis nodded her head in agreement and said, "It is almost 100% certain that Gay lost the key."

"Yes," interjected LaBoche, "my daughter did lose the key, and she did not tell me of it, wishing to spare any anxiety, and that she begged whoever had found it to contact her. She evidently feared that, by giving our address, inquiries would have resulted that would have apprised me of the loss of the key. It was quite logical, quite natural for her to have taken the course she did, for I have been robbed once before."

"Where was that and when," asked Chablis.

"Oh, many years ago, in Cambridge while I was at Harvard. There were stolen from my laboratory the drawings of two inventions that might have made the fortune of the man. Not only have I never learnt who the thief was, but I have never heard even a word of the object of the robbery, doubtless because, in order to defeat the plans of the person who had robbed me, I myself brought these two inventions before the public, giving them away and so rendered the robbery of no avail. From that time on I have been very careful to shut myself in when I am at work. The bars to these windows, the lonely situation of this chateau, this cabinet, which I had specially constructed, this special lock, this unique key, all are precautions against fears inspired by a sad experience."

J. Wayne Frye

Chablis and Lynton in the Room of Doom

Chablis walked to the uniformed officer by the door and said, "Go to the main house please, and ask Mr. Deter who should be there by now, to please come here."

All looked puzzled as to why Mr. Deter was being summoned. Chablis, sensing their intense interest said, "He has found something I think, something that will be of use in the investigation. I went to him yesterday and ask that he search around the lake for a certain item."

Deter strolled into the room and he held in his hand a heavy pair of muddy boots, which he threw on the floor at Chablis' feet. "Way back in the thicket. Covered over by broken branches."

Chablis said, "Do you recognize them Mr. Jacques?"

"Mine, from years ago. I had put them far back in my closet," offered an obviously agitated Jacques.

Then, pointing at a handkerchief in the old man's hand, Bowman said, "That's a handkerchief astonishingly like the one found in the bedroom.

"Yes," said Jacques. They appear almost identical."

"Any comments Mr. Jacques," said Chablis.

"I do not know what to say, except that I would not harm Gay in any way. I love her."

"I know that. I am not accusing you at all. As for the Brooklyn Dodger cap, Mr. LaBoche, were you not born in Brooklyn, and lived there the first 16 years of your life until admitted to Harvard at that young age?"

"Yes, yes I was, and I once had a Dodgers cap?"

"Know where it is?"

"No, I lost track of it over the years."

"Maybe pertinent, maybe not," said Chablis as she shrugged her shoulders.

"The real point here," said a very serious Chablis, "is that I think the intruder wished to disguise his real personality. He did it in a very clumsy way actually, though he thought it smart."

Jacques seemed very nervous, but Chablis walked over to him, looked down, smiled and said, "Don't fret; we are quite sure that you were not the perpetrator. You see, the intruder, no doubt, from the silence around the place, imagined that the moment for action had come. The man who had been able to introduce himself here so mysteriously and to leave so many evidences against Jacques, was, there can be no doubt, familiar with the house. At what hour exactly he entered, whether in the afternoon or in the evening, I cannot say. One familiar with the proceedings and persons of this chateau could choose his own time for entering Ms. LaBoche's bedroom.

"He could not have entered it if anybody had been in the laboratory," offered Marquet.

"How do we know that?" interjected Mr. Brenner.

"There was the dinner in the laboratory, the coming and going of the servants in attendance. There was a chemical experiment being carried on between ten and eleven o'clock, according to Mr. LaBoche, and Jacques who was engaged in assisting. Who can say that the intruder, an intimate, a friend, a stranger or whatever did not take advantage of that moment to slip into the bedroom, after having taken off his boots in the lavatory? Still, there is the escape. That is where the real mystery lies," said Chablis as she walked over to the window and gazed out. "The escape was actually the easiest of all though. Everyone took it for granted that the intruder left the room only by way of the door; it is by the door, then, that the intruder made his way out it must be assumed. At what time, though? At the moment when it was easiest for him to do so; at the moment when it became most explainable, so completely explainable that there can be no other explanation. Let us go over the moments which followed after the crime had been committed. You see, therein, as the saying goes, *lays the rub*."

CHAPTER 8
HE IS BUT DUST AND SHADOW

He assaulted a girl in Cornwall-on-Hudson,
A town not know all that well.
And the day he went to her house
Something sinister was about to dwell.
He strode with a menacing steady walk.
The crime scene was just out of town.
His boots picked up lake dirt off the ground.
Oh, something evil was going down.

He beat her senseless in her bed,
For mercy she did cry,
"Oh my, don't kill me here
I'm not prepared to die."
She begged and pleaded with every word.
He only beat her more and more,
Until upon the floor she fell.
Room of doom is now part of folklore.

He took her by her dark curls,
As he dragged her round and round,
And pounded and pounded her head
His intense anger being fed.
Go down, go down, you poor girl
With the dark and shining eyes;
To the grave Cornwall-on-Hudson girl,
As evil in this cretin's heart lies.

The police came down from town,
But there was no one to put in jail.

Chablis and Lynton in the Room of Doom

All known there seemed to beg pardon,
But sleuths Chablis and Lynton never fail.
Do not get in these two girls way,
For the miscreant will soon be in a cell,
These are the girls with heels from hell,
And all evildoers fear them so well.

Chablis continued her pacing about the room as all eyes gazed upon her lithe frame. She said, "When all four entered the room, Jacques was close to the door, ready to bar the way. There was a moment, during which Jacques was absent as he bent to look under the bed, but Mr. LaBoche should have been able to see the door easily. The moment at which the flight is explainable is the very moment when there were the least number of persons before the door. There was one moment when the Brenner's, Jacques and Mr. LaBoche were all by the bed, but Mr. LaBoche's position facing the door made it impossible for the intruder to escape without him seeing it. When they were all by the bed, from the far side of the bed, the intruder stealthily scooted out from under the bed and made his way silently on tip toes to the door. Here we must admit that Mr. LaBoche had powerful reasons for not arresting, or not causing the arrest of the intruder, since he allowed him to reach the window in the vestibule and later closed it after him. We do not know who committed the crime; we do know now that LaBoche assisted the culprit, though. He harbours a secret. It must be a terrible one, for the father had not hesitated to

J. Wayne Frye

leave his daughter to die behind a door which she had shut upon herself, terrible for him to have allowed the intruder to escape on top of that and to remain silent all this time. There is no other way in the world to explain the intruder's flight from the bedroom!"

The silence which followed this dramatic and lucid explanation was appalling. All present gazed upon LaBoche as he sat staring into space. The man himself, a veritable statue of sorrow, raised his hand with a gesture of resolve. He then pronounced these words, in a voice so loud that it seemed to exhaust him: "I swear by the head of my suffering child that I never for an instant left the door of her chamber after hearing her cries for help; that that door was not opened while I was alone in the laboratory; and that, finally, when we entered the bedroom, the four of us, the intruder was no longer there! I swear I do not know who the intruder was."

All there, except Lynton, looked at Chablis, and seemed to be indicating disgust that she would be so cruel and heartless as to blame a man for complacency in the assault of his own child.

Robert Bowman sighed and said to Chablis. "Nonsense, I cannot believe any of it. You are one of the world's foremost private investigators, but this time you are way off base. This is not believable."

"I had to know Mr. LaBoche, had to know that you did not see the culprit. I had to force your hand, because I felt you harboured a secret and that perhaps this would get it out in the open. I am sorry, but I had to know the truth. I now believe you did not see the culprit."

He looked at her with indignation, but said nothing as he assumed the secret he harboured was safe from discovery. Ah, but he did not know the wiliness of Chablis, who, along with the others left LaBoche there alone in the lab.

As the three of them headed slowly to the car, Robert asked Chablis how she could come to such an incredibly preposterous conclusion with no evidence. He very quietly said, "I understand that the intruder had sought to turn suspicion onto Jacques. Up to that point, you and I are in accord; but no further."

Chablis whispered, "I did all that for a good reason. Come; let us make our way back to the lab."

They skirted the side of the house and went along the pathway to the lab. Night had come. The window in the vestibule was partly open. A feeble light came from it as well as some sounds which drew their attention. The sounds of two people attracted their interest but quickly ceased, then were renewed for a moment, and then they heard stifled sobs. Chablis said, "My whole interrogation was intended to solicit this."

The darkness of the evening seemed to envelop them. Obviously, the conversing pair was in the bedroom. The window in front of them, the open vestibule window remained lit with the faint glow of light from the bedroom. The words were very faint, but they could be comprehended.

"After you."

"No, After you. What have we done? It is all going to come out I am afraid."

Then, Chablis, as the voices became too subdued to understand, said, "It is Mrs. Brenner. I know the voice."

"We should burst in," said Robert.

"No, we need to give them some rope, some leeway. Do not let them know we were here."

"Who is the man in there? I can't make out his voice," said Robert.

"It is LaBoche."

Shocked, Lynton and Robert stared at one another quizzically. Lynton said, "Why, why would those two be meeting clandestinely?"

"That I do not know, and we may not for awhile, but for now, let them have that proverbial rope, because if we interrupt them we may wreck havoc with this case. Let us return to town quietly and make no mention of this knowledge until the right time," said Chablis as they all quietly left.

On the drive back home, Lynton said, "Something has been bothering me about that note you found burned. It said, 'The Presbytery Has Lost Nothing of Its Charm, Nor the Garden Its Brightness.' I am not of this country, and am somewhat ignorant of some of the vernacular."

Robert interrupted her and said, "Not familiar maybe, but no one would ever call you ignorant of anything."

Smiling, Lynton said, "Thank you for the compliment, but in my country the presbytery is the residence of a priest."

"Exactly," interjected Chablis, "And here it is the same or, of course, could apply to the minister's home, as it does not have to be a priest. However, it can also refer to a body of church elders and ministers, especially in the Presbyterian Church. Probably a body of arrogant, pompous, self-righteous hypocrites based upon my experience with religion." She then seemed a bit reticent that she had blurted that last thought out as she said, "Sorry, I have seen little positive in my life from religion."

Lynton laughed and said, "You've seen the poverty and lack of social safety net in my country, which is aided by a church that encourages the poor to keep popping out babies to become wage slaves to the moneyed class. The church does not demand fairness from a government owned by the wealthy. Believe me, Chablis, I, like you, see religion as a huge barrier to the progress of mankind."

Robert, laughing said, "Watch out, questioning religion or capitalism is tantamount to treason in this country."

Chablis winked at Robert as she said, "Just as long as they don't make loving-making a treasonous act."

They dropped Lynton off at the motel as Chablis said to her, "I think I'll get plenty of love-making in just in case they do make it a treasonous act." She drove off with Robert, leaving a smiling Lynton at the curb.

I shall not detail the fornicating pleasure of Chablis and Robert, but needless to say, they both looked a bit haggard at breakfast with Lynton the next day. Lynton pushed the *New York Times* over to the two. It was one of the many newspapers all over the world that were fascinated with the Nobel Price winning scientist's daughter being attacked and put in a comatose state. Of course, the mystery of how the culprit managed to get out of the room was absorbing the minds of many people. It was interesting that all three had all been summoned by Detective Merlin Melson, Robert's underling for a talk about something extremely important.

Arriving at his office, they were all asked to take a seat. "We are getting a lot of pressure from the mayor Robert. He called me this morning and wanted to know where the hell you were, and why you were allowing two private detectives to seemingly run this case."

Robert picked up the phone, dialled the mayor and in a fit of un-subdued anger, "Listen mayor, you think you can do a better job on the investigation, be my guest. Take over the whole damn thing and see how far you get. As for Chablis and Lynton, they have worked some of the biggest cases in the entire world, so I am privileged to have them helping me. Stay out of trying to run my investigation, and I'll stay out of trying to run the city. I suggest you worry about potholes and cutting ribbons at one of your cronies' new businesses. Now, go back to your backslapping, self-promoting constant politicking so you can keep getting elected and not have to get a real job. Goodbye."

Chablis and Lynton in the Room of Doom

As he slammed the phone down, he looked over at Chablis and said, "You're rubbing off on me."

Melson said, "I have been pretty much out of the loop. I appreciate what you told me last night in regards to Mr. LaBoche and Mrs. Brenner, but where are we on this thing? I see no movement toward a solution. I don't see how LaBoche could be involved in his own daughter's assault."

"I'll not swear to anything; Mr. LaBoche has a strangeness that one does not know exactly what to think," said Robert as he looked over at Chablis and Lynton who nodded their heads in agreement about LaBoche's strange behaviour.

"There is one thing that really bothers me," said Lynton. Then she got up, walked over to the window, and as she looked out, continued. "Mrs. Brenner has a strange looking broach that she is always wearing. I did not see her with it on originally, but she has it now, right above her left breast."

"Why would that bother you," asked Melson.

"She keeps rubbing it, almost caressing it. Why?"

Chablis, eased back into the chair, crossing her delectable legs, and said, "I am not sure. I noticed that, too, but whether it is related or not, who knows? This is the most baffling case I have ever untaken."

Lynton said, "*The presbytery has lost nothing of its charm, or the garden its brightness*. It was the phrase which you found on the half-burned piece of paper amongst the ashes in the laboratory. It also had the number 23 on it, and my guess is that it meant October 23. Remember that date, it is highly important. I am now going to tell you about that curious phrase as I did some thinking and research last night while other people were engaged in more delightful activities." She looked over at Chablis and Robert and winked as she continued. "On the evening before the crime, that is to say, on the 22nd, LaBoche and his daughter were at a reception in Manhattan. I found that out on line last night when looking at the *Scientific Journal*. Remember the comment for posterity – *perfume of the lady in black*? It must suffice for you to know that it is a perfume which I have smelled before and smelled again when I walked into that bedroom at the chateau. It is the perfume used to adorn the lip of the stoup where holy water is held."

Robert quickly asked what a stoup was and Lynton explained that it was the container by the entrance to the church sanctuary where holy water is placed so that you can make the sign of the cross after dipping your hand in it. She then continued. "When I smelled that, it reminded me of the previous time I smelled it. It was in the restaurant where we met Conrad Warren. There was a woman in dressed in black wearing a black veil covering her face in the booth behind us. I smelled the same scent, maybe just coincidence, but interesting nonetheless."

"Interesting, but maybe not pertinent, as you intonated," offered Robert.

Chablis said, "I think much hinges on the fact that Ms. LaBoche lost or had her key stolen, and I am surmising that the person with the key had demanded of her something which she had not given him, probably refused to give him. He must have been surprised at the failure of his demand. Finding that his demands would not be met, he elected to foster something sinister and maybe had not even intended to attack her, but came to the chateau for something else that only Ms. LaBoche knows about."

Lynton said, "Your ploy last night obviously motivated a clandestine meeting between Mrs. Brenner and LaBoche, but for what reason, we have not been able to determine, and even if we asked them, the truth is highly unlikely to be forthcoming."

Robert said, "You have been silent Lynton on how you think the culprit might have escaped from the room. Do you have a theory?"

She took her seat again. "I do. I have a theory based on careful thought, but nothing else. But so long as I am not sure of the culprit, I feel it best to keep it to myself for now, for I believe if I revealed it that it might lead others here to get behind my theory when they might have a more plausible one. Anyway, I think you would find my theory a bit absurd at this point."

Chablis, Robert and Lynton went to the chateau, and as they walked about the only sound to be heard was the crunching of the dead leaves beneath their feet. The silence was so intense that one might have thought the chateau had been abandoned. The old stones, the stagnant water of the ditch near the back gate, the bleak ground strewn with the dead leaves, the dark skeleton-like outlines of the tall trees, all contributed to give to the desolate place, now filled with its awful mystery, a most dreary appearance. As they passed round the ditch, they met the Green Man, who did not greet them, but walked by as if they did not exist.

Chablis said, "He is a despicable person. Sometimes there are just people whom you cannot help but dislike, and he is one who breeds contempt."

Lynton interjected, "My dear Wayne says that a person you sometimes perceive as your enemy is but a friend in disguise. Figure that one out."

Chablis and Lynton in the Room of Doom

"Wayne is full of witticisms, and I am often confused by his parables. Yet, I think in this case he means that perception can be wrong, and, in my case, I could be wrong about the Green Man, but I think not. You can sense evil about that man."

Robert looked at Chablis and said, "I can tell you know, suspect at least, who the intruder was."

Smiling, she said, "I can categorically, at this moment, state that I do know him. The mathematical idea I have of the intruder gives results so frightful, so monstrous, that I hope it is still possible that I am mistaken. I hope so, with all my heart, but if I am correct, he is awaiting the right moment to strike again. I want to stay in the chateau tonight with Lynton, Can you arrange it?"

"Of course, it will be no problem I am sure. Let's talk to Mr. LaBoche."

They did so, and the two girls were given adjoining rooms on the ground floor. Around midnight Chablis woke when she heard the cry of a cat ringing out with sinister loudness from the end of the backyard. She rose and opened the window. Cold wind and rain; opaque darkness; and silence greeted her. She reclosed her window. Again, she heard the sound of the cat's weird cry in the distance. She partly dressed in haste. The weather was too bad for even a cat to be turned out in it. What did it mean? Then she thought of that growling cat near the chateau the night of the crime? She seized an umbrella, took her gun from the night table and, without making any noise or alerting Lynton next door, opened the door. The hallway into which she went was well lit. She felt a keen current of air and, on turning, found the window open, at the extreme end of the hallway. Who had left that window open? Or, who had come to open it? She went to the window and leaned out. Five feet below there was a sort of terrace over the semi-circular projection of a room on the ground-floor. One could, if one wanted, jump from the window onto the terrace, and allow oneself to drop from it into the courtyard of the chateau. She merely closed the window, smiling at the ease with which she had built a drama on the mere suggestion of an open window.

Again the cry of the cat broke the quiet. The rain ceased to beat on the window. All in the chateau slept. She walked with infinite precaution on the carpet, making her way to the far end of the hallway. The hallway ended and them there was another hallway running left to right. In front of her were three chairs and some pictures hanging on the wall. What was she doing there she asked herself. Perfect quiet reigned throughout. Everything was sunk in repose. What was the instinct that urged her towards Mademoiselle LaBoche's chamber? Why did a voice within her cry "Go on, open the door and peep in." She cast her eyes down upon the carpet on which she was treading and saw that her steps, almost by instinct, were being directed towards LaBoche's bedroom. On the carpet were traces of footsteps stained with mud leading to his bedroom. Horror! Horror! She recognized in those footprints the impression of the neat boots of the intruder! He had come, then, from without in this wretched night. She quickly scurried back to the window at the end of the hall and looked again. Yes, there it was moved to the left of the window to hide it. There was a ladder.

.

Mr. LaBoche had an anti-room off his bedroom which one had to enter first. Chablis walked in, umbrella in one hand and gun in the other. Under the bedroom door she saw a streak of light. She listened, but there was no sound - not even of breathing! Ah, she thought. "If I only knew what was passing in the silence behind that door! She very quietly tried the doorknob but it was locked and the key turned on the inner side. She was sure that no other crime was being committed, for there was complete silence in the bedroom. There was apparently no harm being done Mr. LaBoche as the door had obviously been opened to admit the intruder and locked behind him.

At the time of the crime in the room of doom, there can be no doubt that she expected the intruder. Was he expected this night? Was it LaBoche who had opened the window for him? All these reflections ran through her brain like a flash of lightning.

Chablis and Lynton in the Room of Doom

As she stood there, she heard the patter of light steps behind her, and looked back over her shoulder. It was Lynton. Chablis put her right index finger to her lips, indicating quiet should be maintained.

Lynton whispered, "It is the same man who broke into Gay's room. I saw the footprints in the hallway. It is possible that there was some reason for the awful silence in the bedroom? Should we intervene?"

"Intervention might do more harm than good," whispered Chablis as she pulled Lynton back away from the door to assure they were not heard.

Now, since the crime, Jacques had been sleeping downstairs in the main house, and Chablis said to Lynton. "Go downstairs and bring Jacques up here, but absolute quiet must be maintained."

Lynton was surprised to find him already dressed. He did not seem surprised to see her. He told her that he had gotten up because he had heard the cry of the cat, and because he had heard footsteps in the backyard, close to his window, out of which he had looked and, just then, had seen a black shadow pass by carrying the ladder from the storage shed, so he decided to get dressed and prepare for any eventuality. They went out together, by a little back door, into the backyard, and stole stealthily along the chateau wall.

Chablis and Lynton in the Room of Doom

She whispered for Jacques to go and get the ladder from the hallway window where it had been used to gain entrance to the chateau. Upon his return, she ordered Jacques to hold the ladder as she climbed up to LaBoche's bedroom window. Taking advantage of a moment when the moon was hidden by a cloud, she moved to the front of the window, out of the patch of light which came from it, for the window was half-open. All she could hear was muffled sounds, as Jacques began to shake the ladder slightly. She looked down and he was motioning for her to climb down, which she did.

Jacques pointed toward the gate keeper's cottage. There was a light on inside the cottage. He whispered. "Why are they up so late? They are always in bed by 9:00 o'clock?"

"My guess is because one of them is in the room with Mr. LaBoche?"

"But why use the ladder? Why not come in the front door and just walk up?"

"Fear of discovery. The two do not want to be seen together."

Meanwhile, Chablis had made her way downstairs and found the two. After chiding Lynton for forgetting her, she understood upon hearing from them all that had ensued. She was about to say something when the subdued, wailing of a cat permeated the darkness. It seemed to have come from close by, only a few metres away. Was the cry a signal? Had some accomplice of the man seen Lynton on the ladder! Would the cry bring the man to the window? Fortunately, it did not.

None of them had any doubt that this was the man from the room of doom. Chablis said, "Jacques, station yourself by the bottom of the stairs. He cannot escape, because the ladder for his escape is gone. Take it down from here also and place it away from the window. Lynton, station yourself at the front door in case, by some means he gets by Mr. Jacques. Do not risk injury by apprehending him; just take note of his looks so that we may identify him. I shall go upstairs with gun drawn and confront him, confront Mr. LaBoche also and finally get to the bottom of this whole affair."

Suddenly, as Jacques was positioning himself and Lynton was moving toward the front door, it began to slowly open. They all stood there waiting, waiting for whoever it was to expose themselves. It was LaBoche. He was not in his room. Lynton immediately put her finger to her lips, indicating he should be quiet. She whispered to him that someone was in his room and they were about to spring a trap. Chablis headed up the stairs, revolver drawn, cocked and ready for any eventuality.

Chablis and Lynton in the Room of Doom

The plan Chablis had formed seemed to be the best, the surest, and the most simple way to apprehend the culprit. Chablis made her way to the door, and gently turned the knob, expecting it to be locked and require her to shoot it off. To her surprise the door was not locked. She was so quiet and so deliberate that the intruder did not hear her at all as he sat at Mr. LaBoche's desk his back turned to Chablis.

At this moment of approaching success, Chablis was filled with anticipatory excitement as she was about to finally see the culprit. The man did not hear her, but obviously sensed her. He rose and she saw the monstrous back of a huge man. He slowly pivoted to his right and turned toward her. He had long hair, a full beard, wild-looking eyes, pale face, framed in large whiskers. To her surprise, she did not know the face.

Like a flash of lighting, he bounded across the room, as she fired her pistol. He managed to hit her arm, pushing it to her right just as she fired. As if she had wings, she picked up her gun, pursued, holding her fire, because she wanted him alive.

He could not escape she thought as he reached the top of the stairwell and bounded down the steps two at a time. He reached the bottom of the stairs where Jacques awaited. Chablis was behind him and Lynton and LaBoche moved forward at the bottom of the stairs. He was trapped.

Suddenly, the man threw Jacques aside with a right arm sweeping motion as if he were a piece of paper. Lynton cocked her right leg, ready to deliver a kick with the heels from hell as LaBoche grabbed the fleeing man's shirt sleeve trying to restrain him. Lynton's kick was met with a powerful, burly hand that caught her heel in mid-air and he lifted her off the floor shoving her sprawling onto the floor. Chablis fired a warning shot assuming that would stop him. It did not. He bounded into the parlour on his left. They all converged on the parlour. They stood there aghast. He was gone!

"Where is he," shouted first Lynton, then Jacques.

"It is impossible he could have escaped!" Chablis cried, seething with anger.

"I touched him!" exclaimed Jacques.

They raced about the room; they tried doors and windows. They were all closed, locked and latched from the inside. They looked at each other in total astonishment. They moved the chairs and lifted the pictures. Nothing, absolutely nothing. Lynton looked down and pointed at some dust on the floor. The moon cast an eerie glow through the window, a shadow of desperation dancing in the semi-darkness. She thought of the culprit: *he is but dust and shadow.*

CHAPTER 8
YOU BETTER BELIEVE IT

Between form and shade without colour,
Between paralysed force and gesture,
Between the idea and the reality,
Between the motion and the act,
Falls the Shadow – the hollow shadow.

Between the conception and the creation,
Between the emotion and the response,
Between the desire and the spasm,
Between the potency and the existence,
Falls the Shadow – the hollow shadow.

There are moments when one feels as if one's brain were about to burst. A bullet in the head, a fracture of the skull and the seat of reason shattered. They were all mystified and bewildered by the latest disappearing act of the phantom from the laboratory room of doom. Chablis bade they all go upstairs and for Mr. LaBoche to survey the room and identify any items that might be missing.

The door was open. Had the phantom not been there to steal but to do harm? By a mere chance, LaBoche had been out. Did that stymie the phantom's real intent?

Chablis walked over to the writing desk, and Lynton sauntered to her side as LaBoche surveyed the room and declared nothing was missing. Ah, but the two intrepid detectives knew there was something missing. Chablis looked at the table and said as she pointed directly at a small writing tablet which had obviously had a page pulled from it. She held it up and you could see intense indentations on the page as if someone had scribbled very hard and left an impression from the page before it that had been torn from the pad.

Chablis looked at LaBoche and said, "You wrote something on the pad and left an impression on the page beneath it. The impression was violently rubbed by the intruder so that he could read what had been written on the previous page. He read it, tore it from the pad and then left the room, found that I was waiting, pushed me aside, looked at the now closed window and knew I had discovered the ladder. He scooted down the stairs, into the room on the left and promptly disappeared into thin air. Mr. LaBoche, we may not be able to solve the vanishing, but we can solve the mystery of what was on the pad. You can tell us that; although I can venture a guess. I pity your daughter, not just for her comatose state, but for what she had endured before the assault. She was living in fear, and you have an idea of what that fear was. She knew that you and Mrs. Brenner were harbouring a secret, a secret that, if exposed, might put all your work at risk. The Brenner's have been here for almost the entire time you have. Why?"

LaBoche bowed his head, and said, "You know more than anyone else, and how you do I cannot comprehend, as I have been so guarded for so many years." He moved to an overstuffed chair, eased into it with a deep sigh and continued. "I was robbed once, and I knew it was not some thief wanting to sell the secrets of my inventions to corporations. I knew the culprit was the U.S. government that has always kept a weary eye on me out of fear that I might share my secrets with a foreign power or refuse to allow them to be used by the military-industrial complex that controls almost every scientific endeavour in the hopes that it can be converted to military use and thereby promulgate the goddamn corporate capitalism that is slowly devouring the world, slowly and surely destroying human kindness so that a few can reap the rewards of a world based on greed. I was prepared to go to Cuba for my work many years ago, where the last vestige of real socialism exists, as Russia and China have completely capitulated to the world of greed, and the U.S. government will not even allow me to travel out of the USA now, not even go into Canada for fear that I might leave with my knowledge."

Lynton said, "Mr. and Mrs. Brenner are here to protect you. They are hired as a buffer between you and the government that wants to control you and your invention that might wind up in the wrong hands, actually the hands of someone who might use it for peaceful purposes."

"Yes, they are ex-agents for the National Security Agency, former spies if you wish. They turned their backs on an agency that is just another one of the cold, calculating, antibodies that permeate the very fabric of our society that is not nearly as free as people think."

"You, then, have endured intense government harassment for years," said Lynton as she shook her head.

"Welcome to America – the land of the free –the delusional free," offered LaBoche.

"You met with Ms. Brenner in your room that night to discuss the theft. You always keep her and her husband informed about what is going on so they can do their job of protecting you from thievery," said Chablis.

"Yes."

"What was on the note pad," asked Chablis.

"Notes on the dissociation of matter."

"So, whoever it was has some important notes on your research," offered Chablis.

"Important, maybe, but not critical. It is information I would gladly put in an article. It is totally insignificant"

J. Wayne Frye

Chablis and Lynton in the Room of Doom

"The intruder does not know that," said Lynton.

"Now, the next question is how did he disappear? There must be a secret passage in that room downstairs," said a perplexed Chablis.

"No, there is absolutely not a secret passage. I would know," said LaBoche, who looked over at Jacques and as he pointed to him, added, "So would he."

Jacques nodded his head agreement and said in a very assured way, "Absolutely no secret passage."

Chablis paced about the room in thought, looked out the window, suddenly turned and said as if she had just experienced a revelation, "He was in disguise. He knew the chateau well, knew his way around it. There is no doubt of that. He simply disguised himself in case anyone saw him, as he wants anonymity."

Chablis walked into the hallway, and said as she looked down at faint footprints left by the slightly wet boots. "See, you notice that those footprints only go in one direction—that there are no return marks? When the man came from the chamber, pursued by all of us, his footsteps left no traces behind them. The mud from his boots had dried, and he moved with such rapidity on the points of his toes, but there was something strange about his flight."

Lynton, with a puzzled look, said "He made no noise."

"Yes," interjected Chablis.

There was a noise from downstairs. They all went to the top of the stairs, looked down and there stood Brenner, gazing upwards and shouting, "What the hell's going on in here? I heard a ruckus, and I saw all the lights on. There is a ladder by the side of the house. What are you all up to?"

"Thank you for your concern," LaBochc said to Brenner.

Chablis moving down the stairs and standing right in front of Brenner said, "You were at the inn, drinking tonight?"

Brenner said, "How did you know?"

Smiling, she replied, "You have a Spanish peanut skin on your jacket. I have been there; they serve peanuts in a big bowl placed on the bar. And, of course, your wife was up very late. That's why the lights were on when I looked out."

Amazed at the skills of detection displayed by Chablis and Lynton, Brenner, skilled former NSA agent, was simply speechless. All he could do was stand in silence and awe.

Chablis and Lynton in the Room of Doom

Lynton said, "You know Mr. Lowman well?"

"I know he is called the green man by people in the village, and that Mr. LaBoche hired him as a gardener. That's about it. He rarely talks to me or anybody else for that matter. He is aloof and uncommunicative."

"He," said Chablis as she sat on the next to the bottom step of the stairs as the others slowly came down, "is only here periodically?"

"Yes."

"Was he here the day of the assault?"

"Yes."

Glancing back at LaBoche who was now standing behind her, leaning on the stair rail, Chablis said, "When Mr. LaBoche's daughter was being assaulted in the room of doom and when he broke open the door and did not find the intruder, what was your initial reaction?"

"Frankly, it crossed my mind that she could have staged the whole thing; otherwise how could anyone have gotten out. How he got out defies all logic. Still, I cannot imagine Ms. LaBoche doing that. There would be no reason for it, none that I could ever come up with at least. I am baffled by the whole affair."

Chablis and Lynton in the Room of Doom

Chablis thought long and hard about his initial theory, but it would make no sense for someone to do all that harm to themselves, put themselves in a coma. No, not feasible.

The evening ended without any explanation of how the intruder had evaded capture, and the conundrum of that room in the château now joined that of the room of doom in the lore of mysteries.

The next day, Chablis and Robert went alone to the room of doom, where she related the previous evening's events. Chablis noticed Robert was seemingly preoccupied as he could not take his eyes off her. He moved over to her, and impulsively took her in his arms. Their mouths hungrily sought one another and the kiss was so long, so lingering that it appeared paramedics might have to be called to administer oxygen. Chablis loosened his pants and in one coordinated move pulled them and his briefs down around his ankles. She dropped to her knees and devoured his member like she had just finished a hunger strike and a huge banquet had been laid before her. She devoured every centremetre of it, working down to the base where she lingered, her nose buried in his pubic hair and she sucked furiously without moving backward, the shaft getting harder and harder as Robert moaned with delight. Then she slowly worked here way back with a sucking motion that no vacuum cleaner could never match in suction power.

J. Wayne Frye

Chablis and Lynton in the Room of Doom

It was as if she was not just sucking his member, but sucking his soul, pulling the very essence of his being from deep within. He was now panting furiously as she knew he was about to explode, so she pumped harder and harder, gobbling it with more and more enthusiasm.

It was then that Lynton walked in, and Chablis, hearing her, with her right hand motioned for her to get out. Chablis needed Robert's joy juice, needed to know she had once again worked her magic on a man. Lynton eased out of the room, closing the door gently so as not to disturb the two frantic lovers.

She stood there thinking of her Wayne, thinking of how he spun his tales of love, and how when she told him of this that he would, no doubt, figure a way to work it into one of his books. She grinned broadly, her succulent lips forming a pouty sensuousness as she thought of how wanton Chablis was. She was the most blatantly sexual person she had ever known, and, for Chablis, sex was not just an act of love. It was a serious recreational activity. Then she heard a drawn out sigh from Robert and knew that Chablis had received the joyous juice of delight that she craved so much. She stood there for awhile, giving them a chance to compose themselves. Then she slowly turned the knob and opened the door only a small amount, peeping in as she said, "May I enter please?"

Chablis and Lynton in the Room of Doom

Chablis said, "Of course."

Lynton opened the door as a sheepish Robert lowered his head while Chablis stood tall and proud. She winked at Lynton as she said, "Didn't your mom tell you to always knock before entering a room?"

"Actually, no," laughed Lynton. Then, as she moved over toward the two, she said, "You two look exhausted. Maybe I should take you down to the inn and buy you a drink."

This time they did not see the landlord, Mr. Lorton, but were received with a pleasant smile by his wife. She spoke in a soft voice. Everything about her expressed gentleness which had not been apparent before. It was obvious that at one time she was a beautiful woman. She had a moderate air of indolence, with great alluring eyes, amorous eyes that know no age limit. There was something in her bearing that was suggestive of despair. She disappeared into the kitchen, leaving on the table a bottle of excellent cider. Robert filled their earthenware mugs. As he did, Lynton said, "I have brought you here for a good reason."

Chablis, without hesitation, said, "You expect the intruder tonight. Am I correct?"

"You are."

Chablis and Lynton in the Room of Doom

Chablis continued. "And please tell us why we should expect him"

"Last night, just as I was going to bed, LaBoche knocked at my room. When he came in he confided to me that he was compelled to go to Manhattan the next day, that is, this morning. The reason which made this journey necessary was at once peremptory and mysterious; it was not possible for him to explain its object to me he said. His anticipation of coming danger overwhelmed him he said. He intonated that there were mysterious and sinister forces lurking about to do great harm. He said that he understood why the examining magistrate thought he might somehow be involved in his own daughter's demise. I told him that I was aware that he knew who the intruder was, and asked why he could not tell me his name. He asked me why I would think that and seemed aghast that I would suggest such a thing. Yet, I think that he knew. I sensed it with all my being."

Robert said, "And he simply avoided your assertion."

"He did," replied Lynton. "And he said that he must leave but he needed to tell me and also to have me convey to Chablis how much appreciated our exceptional intelligence and unequalled ingenuity. But he then asked a service of me and Chablis. He said that perhaps he was wrong to sense something else sinister was afoot, but he was sure there would be another intrusion into the chateau. I promised him we would be on guard in his absence."

Chablis seemed a bit perturbed that LaBoche would go to Lynton rather than her, yet she fully understood that Lynton's quiet, unassuming demeanour might have made him more comfortable.

Robert insisted he be with the two women at the château for safety reasons, but Chablis and Lynton protested that any presence there of the authorities might scare off the intruder. Chablis had been in worse situations and got the OK from Robert who said he'd be by the inn, waiting in his car only a couple of minutes away if needed.

Darkness descended upon the chateau as the two women sent all the servants off to their respective rooms with the admonition to not come into the upper hallway under any circumstances until summoned. Jacques was stationed at the far end of the hallway, around the corner where he could not be seen from any angle. The two intrepid investigators walked quietly by LaBoche's room. Lynton went to the far left, placed herself behind a huge urn and sat on the floor while Chablis moved across the hallway, opened the door to another bedroom, and put the door just ajar enough to where she had a complete view of the hallway.

Chablis and Lynton in the Room of Doom

In the hallway, all the lights were turned off so as to entice the intruder. All three waited impatiently, but were carful to not even breathe too loud for fear of detection.

Chablis briefly stepped into the hallway and motioned for Lynton to join her. They stood in complete silence behind the slightly ajar door and Chablis removed her revolver from her thigh holster, cocked it and stood at the ready. There was a palpable tenseness in the air.

At the stroke of ten Chablis told Lynton to tip-toed across the hallway to LaBoche's room and hide in the closet. Chablis whispered, "In case I miss take this," as she handed her a second pistol she had in the left pocket of her pants. Lynton violently shook her head and pointed down to her heels, known as the high heels from hell which had dispatched many a miscreant over the years, and had been made famous in Wayne Frye's book that was later made into a hit Filipino movie – *LYNTON WALKS ON WATER*. Chablis nodded her head and said, "Be careful, don't take any chances."

.

Chablis embraced her; and then gave her a slight push out the door. Astonished by her embrace, and somewhat disquieted by it, Lynton arrived at LaBoche's room without difficulty, realizing that Chablis felt something bad was about to happen. That was the reason for the affectionate embrace.

Chablis and Lynton in the Room of Doom

Lynton retired into the dark closet. With the door slightly ajar she could see along the whole length of the room. Nothing, absolutely nothing could pass there without her seeing it. But what was going to pass there? Chablis' embrace came back to her mind as she thought that people don't part from each other in that way unless something important or dangerous is about to occur. Did Chablis sense impending doom?

She waited about an hour, and during all that time saw nothing unusual. The rain, which had begun to come down strongly for about an hour had now ceased. It was not more than half-past eleven when someone rounded the area where Jacques was stationed. Where was he thought Lynton and Chablis?

Suddenly, there was a low meowing sound outside. Then it became intense and almost ear shattering. Directly afterwards into the room stepped a cloaked figure, his back towards Lynton and he was bending over the writing desk. When he opened the drawer of the desk and picked up a small package, he turned towards the dark closet, and then she saw who he was. He was the grounds-keeper, the Green Man. As the cry of the cat reverberated about, he put down the package and went to the window. She dared not risk making any movement, fearing she might betray her presence. She thought that Chablis would soon dart across the hall and apprehend him.

Chablis and Lynton in the Room of Doom

Arriving at the window, he peered out into the darkness. The night was now light, the moon showing at intervals. The Green Man raised his arms twice, making signs which she did not understand; then, leaving the window, he again took up his package and moved outside the room. Where was Chablis, thought Lynton?

She moved into the hallway, following the man quietly and Chablis stepped into the hallway too, putting her index finger to her lips indicting quiet must be maintained. The man reached the landing and descended the stairs leading to the room where the previous disappearance had occurred. They looked to their left and saw some large black shoes sticking up around the corner. They quickly moved toward them and there was Jacques, unconscious, obviously rendered that way by a blow to the head. Lynton cradled him in her arms and indicated she would attend to him while Chablis pursued the shadowy figure of the Green Man. Lynton quietly got a cup of water from the bathroom and poured it on Jacques head. He opened his eyes and rose up. "Go, go help Chablis. I am OK."

There comes a time when you think your patience and devotion to duty will finally pay off, but a confluence of events suddenly makes you realize that the best laid plans can fall prey to that ever present fly in the ointment – fate. This would be one of those times.

Chablis and Lynton in the Room of Doom

The Green Man stumbled, tumbled, rolled down the stairs, but never tarried as he hit his feet at the bottom, never slowing as he headed for the front door. He was through it, onto the driveway heading for the gate as Chablis shouted, "freeze or I'll blow your fucking brains out."

Still, he never slowed as she took aim, fired off two rounds at his legs, knowing she must have hit him with at least one shot. He never slowed and fled up the street by the outside wall. She decided she would have to do more than aim at his legs, so she took careful aim at his left shoulder, but as she was about to pull the trigger she suddenly heard the report of a gun to her left and saw the red flash of light indicating it came from behind a clump of trees. Joe Lowman was sprawled on the sidewalk face down. Chablis had seen it too often, she knew he was dead, no doubt about it. There was no need to look at him. He was beyond help.

She turned to her left, kept her gun levelled toward the clump of trees, moving slowly as she noticed Mrs. Brenner moving up the street behind her on the opposite side of the street. Why had she crossed the street she thought, as Mrs. Brenner made her way toward the Green Man. A quick look around the area in the slight quarter moonlight showed one thick boot print on the ground. The shot had, no doubt, been fired by the same person who had been in the room of doom. It was too dark to thoroughly survey the area.

Chablis and Lynton in the Room of Doom

Chablis made her way over to Mrs. Brenner who was leaning over Lowman. She looked up at Chablis and said, "He is dead."

"Of course he is. He had to be silenced."

Jacques and Mr. Brenner came up and Chablis directed them to leave the body where it was and call the police. Nothing was to be touched. The ensuing investigation led by Melson and Bowman offered no clear explanations as when Chablis reached into his pockets the package Lynton had seen him take from LaBoche's bedroom desk was gone. Where could it have disappeared to thought Chablis and Lynton?

The night faded into day and at sun up they examined the entire area again. Moving into the clump of tall trees and bushes they noticed something Chablis was unable to comprehend in the darkness. They found two distinct sets of footprints, made at the same time. They were made by two persons walking side by side. One pair just disappeared and the other led to the street where they stopped at the sidewalk. It was about 6:00 AM, and they were all surprised to see Lynette Richelieu walking up the street with her cat by her side. They greeted her and Robert asked why she was out walking so early. She turned, pointed back toward the cemetery maybe 200 metres away and said, "I spent the night talking to my daughter."

Robert said, "What time did you pass this way last night."

Smiling, she said, "About the time Lowman was shot. Guess I'll have to get a new boarder now. There goes $400 a month. Of course, he didn't pay me regularly anyway."

Surprised at her admission that she had seen the shooting, Chablis interjected. "You saw Lowman shot?"

"Of course, you shot at him, but you ain't a very good shot are you? It didn't stop him, but the black phantom got him for sure."

"The black phantom," asked Robert with a quizzical look as he continued. "What I mean is who is the black phantom?"

"The guy I saw go into the bushes when I walked by and looked over my shoulder when I heard all the commotion. He ran into the bushes with someone else, a short person. The one in black was carrying a pistol. Had it in his right hand. Saw it clearly in the moonlight. You wouldn't know anyone wants to rent a room would you? Don't guess Joe will be needing it now. Maybe he can get a nice spot beside my daughter up in the cemetery. It's nice up there you know. She'd like the company, but Joe ain't a very nice person to associate with."

Chablis and Lynton in the Room of Doom

Chablis, very calmly walked over, placed her hand on Ms. Richelieu's shoulder and said, "We need your help. Tell us all that you saw."

"Oh you mean the black phantom? I saw him plenty of times. Seen him hanging around here twice before – once the night when that pretty young lady was assaulted and a while later when he was just standing over there in the same bushes looking at the chateau."

A very nervous acting Robert said, "Did you see his face?"

"No."

Then, Ms. Richelieu pointed at Jacques who was standing beside Robert and said, "Him. I saw him walking down the road with the black phantom."

"Preposterous," shouted the surprised Jacques as Ms. Richelieu turned her back on them all and pointed toward the cemetery. She, in an almost whisper, said, "There, that is where the lady in the black veil goes. She floats about the cemetery late at night. Oh my, she sings softly too, sings of morose things, things that make your heart cold with doubt that there is any justice in the world, any hope for humanity."

Chablis looked at Robert and they shook their heads. Ms. Richelieu was gone – gone to that land where fantasy is more real than reality. She started wondering back toward the cemetery singing:

"She walks these hills in a long black veil,
When the night winds wail.
Nobody knows, nobody cares, nobody but me.

There was no need to question her further as she was now lost in her fantasy world. Chablis sighed and turned to Jacques. "So, you knew the black phantom to which she was referring?"

"I do not. The woman is crazy. You know that."

Robert said, "Yes, unfortunately we do." He shrugged his shoulders and looked at Chablis. "Don't we?"

"Yep," said Chablis, but one could see those wheels turning in her head. Was Ms. Richelieu crazy? Yes, but the crazy can often be more sane than the so-called sane she was thinking. She walked back to the chateau with the others, looked back over her left shoulder at the clump of trees where the shot that had felled the Green Man came from. She then glanced over at Lynton, moved closer and whispered, "You and I are about to blow this case wide open aren't we?"

Lynton whispered back, "You better believe it."

CHAPTER 10
CHAVAZ AND VINAS WILL DAZZLE YOU

Shadows in the darkness haunt hope
Evil intentions fly about like a bat
Life hangs by a slender rope
Ah, hear the wailing cry of the black cat

Where had the package been dropped? They all frantically looked for it to no avail, finally giving up. The next day, LaBoche came back from the hospital with grand news – his daughter had blinked her eyes. It was surmised by all, after reflection, the death of the gardener, who had likely been allied with the intruder, or maybe had even been the intruder himself, had paid the ultimate price for his treachery as apparently his compatriot had silenced him forever.

Chablis said to LaBoche, "What was in the packet you had on the desk?"

"Formulas in regards to the dissociation of matter, but valuable only," then he stopped and you could see consternation grow on his face, "if put with the other documents that were stolen earlier."

"It was pretty careless of you to leave them where they were easily accessible. Almost as if you did not care if they were stolen," offered Lynton.

Robert stood silent, as if in some kind of trance, with a look of deep concern on his face as Chablis and Lynton seemed more in charge than he was. Chablis said to LaBoche, "You were in Manhattan, but obviously stopped by to check on your daughter before coming home."

"Yes."

"Did you ever suspect Lowman of nefarious deeds?"

"No, absolutely not. He was a horrible person, but a credible gardener," said LaBoche.

"What were you doing in Manhattan Mr. LaBoche," asked Lynton as she sighed and continued. "It is crucial that we know."

LaBoche remained silent for a long time, just staring down at the floor. Then he blurted out, "None of your business."

"Listen to what I am about to say," Chablis said in a low tone, "and let it give you confidence. You do not know the name of the intruder. However, you thought Mrs. Brenner knew it. That is why she was in your room that night. Why did you believe she knew it?"

"Because she had work for the NSA, and I assumed they had arranged the theft,"

Chablis and Lynton in the Room of Doom

"Why wouldn't they have just taken it themselves?"

"You know the way these slimy government bastards work. Come on, they had to make it look good, make it look like someone else had broken in and stolen the information. Our government is the worst enemy the people have, not some foreign government or some terrorist organization. The biggest terrorist organization in this country is the government and the corporations that own it."

Lynton chimed in, "Not much different than the Philippines."

Chablis said, "Well, the package of papers was not valuable unless they had the earlier information. Seems almost as if you wanted the information stolen Mr. LaBoche."

"Preposterous."

Chablis sighed, as she offered an observational analysis. "There never has been a case with so many obscure, incomprehensible and inexplicable points."

Marquet had showed up at the chateau and listened intently as Chablis continued. "Strange you would show up Mr. Marquet, because I was about to have Robert call you. The evidences are, in appearance, so overwhelming against you right now that I am frankly surprised you have not been arrested, though I believe, despite evidence that points in your direction, you were not the intruder."

Stiffening himself, Marquet shouted, "Certainly I was not the intruder."

"The attempt on Ms. LaBoche's life and the killer of Lowman were committed by the same person," said a confident Chablis. "I will name that person at 6:00PM tomorrow. I must wait until then for a very good reason."

Robert, having stood silent, now seemed incensed. "Chablis, I've had enough of this bull-shit. You and Lynton have both been playing Sherlock and Watson, and I am tired of it. Why must we wait?"

"Well, that I cannot explain right now, but you will understand it tomorrow at 6:00. I can, however, give you now some explanation of the murder of the groundskeeper. I think all here would agree that the killer of Lowman, the Green Man, was also Ms. LaBoche's assailant, but we are not agreed as to how the intruder escaped that night from the room of doom. You see, there was a woman in a long black veil seen wandering about. Ms. Richelieu referred to her as the lady in the black veil, and others have called her the dark phantom."

Chablis and Lynton in the Room of Doom

Robert seemed to be growing more impatient. "Chablis, please, I am bewildered."

"Oh, aren't we all? You see, the Green Man, Mr. Lowman, has many lady friends, and he often accompanied Ms. Richelieu on her walks to the cemetery, but left her alone there as he roamed about before walking home. It was there he met the lady in the black veil. This lady had a husband who was usually sound asleep or passed out from too much drink. She met him clandestinely in the garden shed by the gate of the chateau. It was there they engaged in lovemaking."

"How on earth," said Robert, "do you know all this?"

Lynton offered the explanation. "We went into the shed yesterday, and found there a pile of dust on a shelf and on it was the indentation of a veil – the little marks made by the lace in the dust. As for Lowman, that is supposition, but pretty solid as we had talked to Ms. Richelieu and she said that Lowman would occasionally accompany her, then just disappear. The shed, Lowman being about and having access to it is, as I said, supposition, but a pretty solid supposition."

"Who is the lady in the black veil?" asked Robert.

"Mrs. Lorton," replied Chablis.

Chablis and Lynton in the Room of Doom

"What," shouted Robert.

"Well, at first," said Lynton as she looked over at Mrs. Brenner, who had wandered over to the foyer sofa and taken a seat, "we thought it was Mrs. Brenner and you meeting there, because of the meeting we overheard your daughter's bedroom, but now we know that had nothing to do with romance."

"Mrs. Lorton came to the chateau the night of the assault. She and her husband were here so quickly because she was already here meeting Lowman and her husband had followed Lowman here to catch the two in their dalliance. She, enveloped in a large black shawl which served also as a disguise, was the phantom that has been alluded to. She is a Mohawk Native American and knows how to imitate the mewing of a cat and she would make the cries to advise Lowman of her presence. We confirmed her heritage by checking her birth certificate yesterday. Previous to the tragedy in the room of doom Mrs. Lorton and Lowman had left together, but had run into Mr. Lorton. I learned," then she looked over at Lynton and corrected herself. "We learned of these facts from an examination of the footmarks around the shed. Lorton confronted them outside the gate and there was a scuffle. You, of course, will remember Robert when we went to the inn, Mr. Lorton had very strong feelings against the Green Man. And it was for good reason. Who would not hold a grudge against a man who was fornicating with his wife? There is always that inner urge in us all for the forbidden fruit. Mrs. Lorton sought it in the arms of the Green Man. Perhaps religion is the culprit as it spends an inordinate amount of time telling us all what we should not do. Then again, religion is not on trial here is it?"

Chablis continued. "Now, this is all supposition, but based upon a pretty solid review of the facts. While the two men were scuffling, they heard the shots from Gay's room. In the confusion, Lowman ran off into the darkness, and Mr. and Mrs. Lorton ran to the chateau to see what had occurred, forgetting their tête-à-tête over Mrs. Lorton's infidelity for awhile. That explains why they were here so quickly."

Chablis walked over to Mrs. Brenner, stood right in front of her, and looking down at her feet, said, "We have all been looking for a man as the intruder, but what if it was a woman? You have rather large feet for a woman don't you Mrs. Brenner? Don't worry, it is O.K., because Mrs. Lorton is a size 11, also very large feet for a woman. There is a reason for that."

Everyone there stood in awe, as Chablis looked over at Robert and said, "Please have all the interested parties assembled here tomorrow at 6:00 PM, and Holmes and Watson, excuse me, Chavez and Viñas, will dazzle you with the conclusion of the case.

CHAPTER 11
THE CASE WAS OVER OR WAS IT

Dark clouds filled with rain
dance in the purple sky.
Rain is a cloud- falling apart,
pouring its shattered pieces down.
Ah, but is this all that falls apart?
Evil can be shattered as well.
Our intrepid investigators are dancing too.
This case they are now about to undo!

Robert, perplexed and bewildered, for reasons that will become clearer soon, assembled all the parties concerned in the case. It is impossible to adequately describe the tense excitement which appeared on every face, as Chablis and Lynton made their way into the room of doom where all had been assembled.

"This mystery," said Chablis as all were seated in straight back chairs that had been brought into the room to accommodate the assemblage, "was easily solvable from the very beginning if we had simply used some common sense and logic."

Lynton walked over to the barred window, stood there looking out for awhile and then turned to face those assembled. "It was impossible for the intruder to get away without being seen at the time you all think the crime occurred. That is the key – the time you think it occurred. Those present that night at the chateau or near the chateau, included: Jacques, the Brenner's, the LaBoche's, Mr. Marquet, Ms. Richelieu and Mr. Deter."

Robert, very perturbed, shouted, "Who is the culprit? Who? You are here to reveal him."

"We are. Just be patient. Melson arranged to have operatives keep an eye on all except those here at the chateau which Lynton and I observed all day, assuming there would be an attempt to skedaddle, head out away from certain apprehension. Obviously, the culprit is smarter than we are, or at least thinks he is. That is why all this really came about. He wanted to prove he was smarter than I was – and Lynton, too."

Lynton said, "We do know though that the culprit artfully used disguise. In fact, he or she has been a master of disguise for years. The culprit is an incredibly sinister individual who works for the C.I.A. The person is only known as *the shadow*. *The shadow* spends years if necessary assessing a situation before striking. It had been reported by the C.I.A. that this shadowy figure had died in glorious service to his country, but he or she had not done so." She then looked at LaBoche. "You knew of this person."

"I did. I did! I was told by the government that no matter where I was that they would find me, because *the shadow* would never lose sight of me.

J. Wayne Frye

Chablis and Lynton in the Room of Doom

They told me that every time I looked over my shoulder he might be there, lurking in darkness."

"And they were right," said Chablis as she walked about the room. "You were an anomaly, because you could not be bought."

Lynton said, "That is something very few people understand, an individual who cannot be bought. It is said we all have our price, but they could not find your price. You were beyond reproach. That makes you a severe threat Mr. LaBoche."

"You see," interjected Chablis, "this is only partially about controlling you Mr. LaBoche, but in order to do that the government has placed the Brenner's, whom you thought had retired from the NSA but had not, and who knows how many others to watch you, keep an eye on you to always be sure that your inventions do not tread on corporations and the government which wants to assure that it can always control other nations in the all-fired war to keep capitalism afloat so that the entire world can be enslaved to serve the 1% who rule with impunity."

"What do you mean partially control?" asked Robert.

"Remember the key Gay lost? We thought that was going to be resolved without telling her father once she got it back. Truth is she never lost the key. It was stolen by the intruder. However, Gay wanted it stolen. She knew he needed to get into the house to get into that cabinet in the laboratory. Ms. LaBoche actually let him in through the front gate to circumvent anyone else who might see him in order to get the key back, but she had her own plans far beyond the mere retrieval of a key and they were nefarious too. In fact, they included murder. The key was never lost really. You see, Gay wanted it stolen when she was at the library that day. I questioned the librarian."

Lynton gave her a stern look and Chablis continued. "I mean we questioned the librarian, and low and behold, there was a man with a white beard there that day when Ms. LaBoche was also there. He fit the description of the very man we chased down the stairs who disappeared in the parlour. The librarian took notice of him became he sat right next to Ms. LaBoche. It seemed unusual to her that he would sit so close to her, when the library had many empty tables. She inferred that the man looked as if he were wearing a fake beard. It seemed he was in disguise. Then, she noticed that Ms. LaBoche went into the stacks, leaving her purse obviously at the table. The culprit thought he was being smart in lifting the key, but Gay knew it would be stolen. Anyway, the librarian saw the bearded man walk outside and meet another man – the Green Man. They engaged in a frantic conversation and left together.

J. Wayne Frye

You see, Mr. LaBoche, my guess is that the Green Man, Mr. Lowman, was also a government agent. This whole nefarious affair is wrapped up in a government plot to make sure it had all your information in regards to the dissociation of matter at its fingertips, ready to use it in its never ending endeavour to secure the world for corporate capitalism, American style. The U.S. government is certainly not your friend in this affair."

"You are saying my daughter set-up the meeting with the intruder? Actually let him in without realizing his real intentions"

"I am. Some very smart people are often very naïve. Your daughter's naïveté was catastrophic."

Lynton chimed in. "In fact, your daughter offered herself up for murder without realizing it. She agreed to meet the man when she knew you would be out Mr. LaBoche. The intruder needed to kill her to be sure his nefarious intentions were not discovered, but he, himself, was a bit incompetent in carrying out his plan."

Robert said, "Preposterous."

"Really?" replied Chablis a she stared intently at Robert. "About as preposterous as you being a government agent also, being recruited by the CIA to make sure that the investigation did not lead directly to Washington, D.C. and the slimy bastards who talk about freedom while destroying it every day."

Just as Robert was about to protest, Lynton placed her right hand in front of her chest, making a stopping motion and said, "Be careful – 'me thinks you protest too much.' We talked to Detective Melson who said you had been meeting with the F.B.I." She then pointed toward the door and there stood Melson smiling. Lynton continued. "He is here in earnest to make an arrest, because frankly, you are not to be trusted Robert."

LaBoche asked, "But even if she let him in. How did he get out of that room without being seen?

"Easy," replied Chablis.

Lynton could not resist. "He wasn't in the room." She then made a deferral motion with her right hand toward Chablis.

You could tell Chablis was really enjoying herself. "While Mr. LaBoche and Jacques were away, as I said, she let the intruder in to get the key and pay for its return, or that is what the intruder thought. She was probably not shocked to see it was the bearded man from the library, but still she wanted the key and felt it a necessity to let him accompany her to her room as he insisted he would not transact business anywhere else."

Chablis and Lynton in the Room of Doom

"Now, this man had killed before at the behest of the government he serves. A young woman named Adele Richelieu lived here in relative anonymity with her mother. You see, Adele was on the government's hit-list, because she had once worked with a Harvard professor and his daughter on a top secret project. Yes, she had worked with you Mr. LaBoche had she not?"

"Many years ago, yes. We had no idea she lived here when we bought the château. She asked us to keep her presence here a secret as she had turned her back on working for the bastards."

"That is why," offered Lynton, "that you were in Manhattan recently. I have it from a very good source that you have been meeting with a Park Avenue private detective who is trying to find her killer. You felt sorry for Ms. Richelieu and wanted to ease her pain."

"Yes."

"You thought you owed it to her mother to find the killer. The truth is you do not trust Robert to investigate it, as it has been three years and not one single clue has been found." Staring intently at Robert, she continued, "I would say that was a good reason not to trust him to find the killer."

"You mean that my daughter's attacker killed Adele Richelieu?"

"Oh, he did and for what the U.S. government thought was a very good reason. You see, they found out she was here, and they assumed she had been in contact with you, probably working on the dissociation of matter with you and your daughter. So, one night when she was on her walk, the same man who attacked Ms. LaBoche, was sent to interrogate Adele Richelieu about any association with you. The interrogator used a method he had learned while he was an interrogator at Guantanamo, where America refined torture to a high art. Now, what do Muslims find abhorrent? Of course, they are repulsed by pigs. At Guantanamo, ham bones were used to beat the detainees."

All present were astonished as Chablis said, "Yes, the weapon used on Adele was a ham bone, the same ham bone that would later be used in an attempt to kill Ms. LaBoche. There is a thread of deceit leading right back to Washington in all that has occurred here."

Lynton said, "The U.S. government could have cared less about the man's predilection for murder, as they were only interested in his ability to procure the information they needed that the Brenner's were unable to obtain."

Again Lynton made a dramatic hand motion toward Chablis, who continued. "As I said, when the three men, Brenner, Jacques, LaBoche went into the room, with Mrs. Brenner in the doorway, and looked for the intruder, he was not there because he was not in the room. You see, what happened was well planned. All along the intention was to murder Ms. LaBoche and steal the papers in the laboratory cabinet, but Gay had her own plan, too."

Chablis walked, no paced about the room, as she continued. "Why did we all assume the intruder was in the room when it was opened? Because he left his tracks in the room? Good! But may he not have been there before the room was locked. Let us look into the matter of these traces and see if they do not point to my conclusion, our conclusion. The simple fact is that the intruder had been in the room before. It was necessary for me to reconstruct the occurrence and make of it two phases, each separated from the other, in time, by the space of several hours. One phase in which Ms. LaBoche had really been attacked, the other phase in which those who heard her cries thought she was being attacked. What were the marks on Ms. LaBoche? There were marks of strangulation and the wound from a hard blow on the temple. The marks of strangulation were hidden by her as were the blows to the temple, which she hid by braiding her hair.

Chablis then looked over at LaBoche and asked, "She wore a high collar blouse that night did she not?"

"Yes."

"She wore it to conceal the marks from an attempt to strangle her."

"But why would she not say something about the assault?" asked LaBoche.

"She was scared to reveal who it was, because she felt it incumbent upon her to hide his identity from you. Anyway, she had her own plans for the culprit. She had actually lured him here to kill him, which I shall explain shortly. My guess is that Ms. LaBoche has been in danger at the hospital, but Robert here could not contravene Detective Melson's authority in that regards, so she has been protected 24/7."

Robert started to move toward the door very deliberately. Melson, standing there, put his hand on his coat as if to let Robert know he was packing and said, "Don't Robert."

"But surely she was horribly injured. Why would we not have noticed?" asked Jacques.

"I could not explain the blow on the temple. I understood it even less when I learned that the mutton-bone had been found in her room. She could not hide the fact that she had been struck on the head, and yet that wound appeared evidently to have been inflicted during the first phase, since it required the presence of the intruder who fled when he was wounded, thinking that discretion is the better part of valour. She was not aware of how severe her head wound was. She was headed toward a coma, but did not know it. She covered up the wound by arranging her hair in bands on her forehead. As to the mark of the hand on the wall, that had evidently been made during the first phase when the intruder was really there. All the traces of his presence had naturally been left during the first phase; the mutton-bone, the black footprints, the cap, the handkerchief, the blood on the wall, on the door, and on the floor. If those traces were still all there, they showed that Gay LaBoche, who desired that nothing should be known of her assault, had not yet had time to clear them away. This led me to the conclusion that the two phases had taken place one shortly after the other. She had not had the opportunity, after leaving her room and going back to the laboratory to her father, to get back again to her room and put it in order. Her father was all the time with her, working. So that after the first phase she did not re-enter her chamber till midnight. Jacques was there at ten o'clock, as he was every night; but he went in merely to close the blinds and light the nightlight. Otherwise the room was dark, so he could not have seen anything, as the night light was very minimal. Owing to her disturbed state of mind she had forgotten that Jacques would go into her room. I think she was not aware that so many evidences had been left. After she had been attacked, she had only time to hide the traces of the man's fingers on her neck and to hurry to the laboratory. Had she known of the bone, the cap, and the handkerchief, she would have made away with them after she had gone back to her chamber at midnight. She did not see them because she was suffering from a concussion as a result of the horrible blow to her head, and remember that she undressed by the uncertain glimmer of the night light. She went to bed, worn-out by anxiety, fear and the coming coma that would be induced by not seeking medical help immediately."

"Plausible," said LaBoche with a deep sigh. "And what of the two shots we heard and her screams?"

"When Gay was alone in the room shouting, the struggle and noise that were heard is simply that in her nightmare of pain which suddenly overwhelmed her, making her thrash about the room in agony. She was haunted by the terrible experience she had passed through in the afternoon. In her near coma induced dream she sees the intruder again about to spring upon her and she cries for help, cries out murder. Her hand wildly seeks the revolver she had placed within her reach on the night-table by the side of her bed, but her hand, striking the table, overturns it, and the revolver, falling to the floor, discharges itself, the bullet lodging in the ceiling. I knew from the first that the bullet in the ceiling must have

J. Wayne Frye

resulted from an accident. Its very position suggested an accident, and fell in with our theory of a nightmare from the concussion and coming coma. We no longer doubted that the attack had taken place before Gay had retired for the night. After wakening from her frightful dream and crying aloud for help, she had fainted. Now, based on the evidence of the shots that were heard at midnight, there were two shots, one which wounded the intruder at the time of his attack, and one fired at the time of the nightmare. There were not two shots fired then, one shot had been fired earlier causing the wound, the second shot that night was not fired in the room at all. When a shot is fired, especially in a closed room, the enclosure is like an echo chamber. The report was simply one shot fired, but the echo affect from everything being tightly, almost homiletically sealed in that tight room created the perfect conditions for two shots being heard.

Jacques interrupted. "But why did we not hear the shot in the afternoon?"

"Ah, the shot was muffled," offered Lynton.

"Yes," said Chablis. "You see, there as a struggle for the gun, and the report was muffled. The injury occurred then. The hand was actually put over the gun. The shot wounded the hand of the murderer, actually his wrist, and had caused it to bleed down his arm so that he left the bloody imprint on the wall. The second shot in the ceiling everyone heard was the accidental shot during the nightmare which included an echo."

Chablis ordered the door closed and the blinds pulled down. She reached into her pant's pocket, removed what she explained was a blank cartridge, put it in her gun and fired toward the ceiling. There was an immediate echo.

"Now," said confident Chablis as she signalled for the door to be opened again, "back to the wound on the temple. It was not originally physically severe enough to have been made by means of the mutton-bone. The real, nearly fatal blow must have been made during the second phase. It was to find this out that we went back here and obtained my answer. This whole case," and then she looked directly at Robert, "was intentionally handled incompetently."

Chablis drew a piece of white folded paper from her blouse pocket, and drew out of it an almost invisible object which she held between her thumb and forefinger. "This is a very minute hair, a dark black hair like Ms. LaBoche's. I found it sticking to one of the corners of the overturned table. The corner of the table, hardly visible it was; but it told me that, on rising from her bed, in a frenzy caused by the original blow which caused a concussion, Gay had fallen heavily and had struck her head on the corner of the table's marble top. That was the real blow, the blow that sealed her fate – put her in what, unfortunately, doctors assume is an irreversible coma. In a stroke of irony, she hit her head in almost the same spot where the original blow by the ham bone had been struck; thereby, making it appear there was only one wound area."

She looked over at poor Mr. LaBoche and realized she had been too fatalistic as he lowered his head. She uttered, "I am sorry to be so blunt."

Lynton walked over and put her arm on LaBoche's shoulder as Chablis continued, "We still had to learn, in addition to the name of the intruder, the time of the original attack. The intruder had introduced himself into the area between five and six o'clock. At a quarter past six Mr. LaBoche and his daughter had resumed their work. At five Mr. LaBoche had been with his daughter, and since the attack took place in his absence from his daughter, I had to find out just when he left her. Mr. Brenner admitted to me in an interview that he held a brief conversation with Mr. LaBoche about that time, a little after 5 in his cottage. Gay was not with them he emphatically stated. Gay who had the revolver ready by her bedside to dispatch this person she hated. Meanwhile, her attacker was carrying a hambone on him, ready to deliver a blow for freedom and the good old American way. What passed must have taken place very quickly. Gay tried to call for help; but the man had seized her by the throat. Her hand had sought and grasped the revolver and as the intruder was striking her on the head with the mutton-bone, she fired in time, and the shot wounded the hand that held the ham bone. The bone fell to the floor covered with the blood of the murderer, who staggered, clutched at the wall for support—imprinting on it the red marks and, fearing another bullet, fled. She saw him pass through the laboratory, and listened. He was not long at the window. At length he jumped from it. She flew to it and shut it. The danger past, all her thoughts were of her father. Had he either seen or heard? At any cost to herself she must keep this from him. Thus, when Mr. LaBoche returned, he found the door of the room of doom closed, and his daughter in the laboratory, bending over her desk, at work. All seemed right with the world, but inside Gay's head was a ticking time bomb ready to explode at almost any time.

Turning towards Robert, she cried: "You know the truth! Tell us, then, if that is not how things happened. Tell us how you purposefully botched the whole investigation in service to those cretins in Washington who are nothing but slimy, creepy servants of the capitalist class."

"I, I, I," uttered Robert as Chablis cut him off and said, "No need to reply. There is no reply to justify your service to the bastards who bow and scrape before the moneyed class to serve them rather than the people they are supposed to serve.

J. Wayne Frye

Chablis and Lynton in the Room of Doom

Everything was purposefully used to point to Jacques. He was an easy fall guy, but no one really bought it did they. That was the fly in the ointment. You faked helping me and Lynton, because we have a reputation for being un-ravellers of mysteries. You were damn scared all of a sudden. So complicated a scheme as this must have been long and carefully thought out in advance. On one occasion, the intruder had disguised himself with a long white beard as he did the night he disappeared as we chased him. In this way he had been able before the crime, on two occasions, to take stock of the château, wandering about it outside. He had even managed to lay his hands on the cap, the handkerchief, the boots – anything to point the finger at Jacques. All these items were compromising for Jacques, as even the ball cap could be traced to him, though it belonged to LaBoche, which explains his distress at our sudden appearance in the case.

"Now we come to why the mysterious bearded man showed up that night upstairs. He simply had decided that LaBoche was hiding more of the information as his handlers told him the formulas he had stolen were missing key elements. So, he returned to once again to try and find what those despicable freedom tramplers in Washington were after. We were ready for him, but true to form he disappeared before our very eyes. All the while as this went on, poor Ms. LaBoche lingered in her coma and Lynton and I wondered just why she had gone to such an extreme to not reveal her loss of the keys. You see, she had sacrificed her life, in reality, to not reveal the loss, the theft of those keys."

LaBoche sit up straight, sighed as if actually pleading to hear why all this had felled his beloved daughter. Chablis walked over to him, standing by his chair. "The beginning dates from the time when, as a young girl, she was living with her father, a visitor at the house, a Frenchman, had succeeded by his wit, grace and persistent attention, in gaining her affections before she fell in love with Jacques. The truth was the man was another government plant. Jean Paul Pontere was but one of the many names under which the notorious spy plied his trade. The young, impressionable Gay had fallen in love. To her Jean was everything that her love painted him. She was indignant at her father's disdainful attitude, and continued to see him behind his back until she discovered his real intentions. Then, she threw him over without haste and devoted herself to her father, forsaking all until she found Jacques."

Chablis walked over to Jacques and put her hand on his shoulder. "Of course, we all know her father had decided against her liaison with Jacques and thought Marquet the better match. It was then that some words were scrawled on a piece of paper in the laboratory, not by her father who hid the truth from us, but by her former lover. *The presbytery has lost nothing of its charm, nor the garden its brightness,* described the Harvard church yard where the two had often met during their love affair."

Again, Chablis turned and stared at LaBoche, who bowed his head as he said, "Yes, it is true. I did not want the truth of her affair with that despicable man known by anyone, not even as she lay in a coma. I wanted her to always be looked upon with reverence."

"Now," continued Chablis, "Gay learned who the bearded man was – her former lover in disguise. She actually lured him to the room of doom. Yes, she had intentions to kill the man, rid the world of this despicable slimy creature once and for all. Remember the burlap bags? They were there because she fully intended to dismember his body, cart if off and throw it into the lake. She made it easy for him to steal her keys, because she was overcome with hatred for what he had done. Unfortunately, her plan failed and she found herself at the mercy of this unscrupulous wretch who arrived on the scene a bit too early and unexpected. We all now know the results."

LaBoche let out a sigh as he shook his head in disbelief at the astuteness of these two remarkable women. Yet, he had to ask the question that was on everyone's mind. "But who among us is the intruder? No one has a wound on the hand."

Chablis and Lynton in the Room of Doom

Chablis looked over at Lynton as if to say, "Go ahead and tell them."

Lynton said, "The perfume of the lady in black. I smelled the perfume here at the chateau, because I had smelled it several times before. The lady in black was sitting in a booth near us that day when Conrad Warren asked the two of us to explore the case. See what we could find out. He is a wily fellow; he is. You see, the lady in black is also an accomplished spy."

Lynton continued, "Warren is an egotist and a master at disguise – his favourite is an old man with a long white beard. He has even developed an acceptable persona as a columnist, but his real intentions have always been to serve a government that is dedicated to preserving the status quo and enslaving Americans to the false notion of living in the land of the free. His ego has grown over the years as he has served the nefarious purposes of a government that is as despicable as the politicians who are bought and sold by the merchants of greed. Read his columns and you will see his egotism in everything he writes. Warren is the bearded man. Warren is Jean Paul Pontere, Warren is the intruder and Warren is the killer of the Green Man. He considers himself invincible, and it is his conceit which led him to hire the person he considers the greatest detective alive so he could merely inflate his ego by showing he could even fool her. Though it would have to be kept secret, the person fooling her would have an inflated ego that would soar with euphoria. Hey, he once wrote in his column, *'We are nothing but meat covered skeletons riding a big round rock hurdling through space. Come on, what do we have to fear. We are all dare devils!'* You see, Warren is a dare devil of sorts himself, but he never reckoned that Gay would see through his disguise and try to kill him. Had she not had the revolver there, all would have gone exactly as planned."

"We reflected back on that day we first met Warren, and how when he raised his arm slightly, there was a bandage on his upper wrist. It did not seem significant at the time, but when we reflected back on it and the fact that the woman in black was there, we put two and two together. You see, Gay did not hit the intruder in the hand, but on the upper wrist and the blood trickled down which led to it filling his hand with blood which wound up on the wall. So monstrous was his ego that he actually wanted to hire Chablis and prove to himself that he could outsmart the best. Detective Melson had him arrested a few hours ago. Of course, we all know that he will walk, because the government will shout national security and once again justice will be subverted."

"And the lady in black?" asked Jacques.

"Mrs. Lowman, of course."

Chablis and Lynton in the Room of Doom

Mrs. Lowman stood up, as if she was about to head for the door, but Melson was an imposing figure. She sat back down. The case was over, or was it?

J. Wayne Frye

EPILOGUE
WOULDN'T YOU LIKE TO KNOW

Our minds are full of flammable thoughts,
Filled with fodder for a wildfire.
Breaking down a pile of plans and plots,
Evil entities constantly conspire.

Combustible questions must not be asked.
Justice and fairness we cannot view.
Complacency is promoted as virtue,
As all hope is burned from you.

The blaze that's made burns a greedy world.
It turns old thoughts to dust and ash.
A furious raging, all-encompassing inferno,
Destroys all that's in its path.

But fire doesn't always kill.
Sometimes a few can see into the light
A tool to make us see a better way,
A glow to brighten up the night.

We keep a dangerous company,
For when a conversation sparks,
Maybe it will burn the world,
Or perhaps it merely lights the dark.

You never win battling the U.S. government. The torture chambers that have been used to punish all who defy the biggest terrorist nation on earth, the prisons that house those who dare to challenge authority, the ghettos of despair where people are cast aside as casualties of unfettered capitalism and the manipulation of those who blindly stand with hand over heart pledging allegiance to a lie are all proof that in the never ending battle against fairness and justice, unfairness and injustice always come out on top courtesy of a government that serves the corporations and the wealthy with dedicated devotion. Those arrested that day would never be brought to justice, because there simply was no justice in America. It had long ago been sacrificed at the altar of greed. Chablis and Lynton had looked into the impossible and come up with the probable. Though they understood eventually a government cover-up would allow the culprits to walk free, they felt satisfaction in knowing that they had exposed, at least for awhile, the nefarious dealings of those who served evil. The public would read about it, hear about it, but never really digest it. They would simply shrug their shoulders and accept their inexorable, miserable fate while gleefully sitting on the sofa watching the latest media whores prance around in their finery or shout with euphoria as some moron dunked the ball, hit a homer or threw a touchdown pass. Thus was the dilemma of a world where everything had been dumbed down to placate the masses who were like sheep being led to the slaughter. As one politician gleeful observed, "if God did not want them sheered, he would not have made them sheep."

Chablis and Lynton in the Room of Doom

Channa and Ingrid rejoined their two friends in Manhattan and lamented missing all the excitement. Miraculously, only two days after the case was wrapped up, Gay came out of the coma. Jacques was there by her side, and her father was beaming with joy, knowing that he was going to have a new son-in-law now who would truly love his daughter and show her the affection she deserved. Chablis and Lynton were at the hospital to meet the woman who had been at the centre of all their efforts. Had they waited a few days, she could have identified the culprit herself and a lot of detective work could have been avoided.

Nothing had really been changed by uncovering the mystery, as a government dedicated to conserving the status-quo would continue on its nefarious path, but satisfaction reigned in the minds of Chablis and Lynton. They had proved to be stellar at the art of detecting.

The four girls walked out of the hospital and hailed a cab. As the cabbie weaved and bobbed down Park Avenue, Channa said, "But there is one thing that was not explained. How did the bearded disguised Conrad Warren disappear in that other room on the night you chased him?

Smiling, Chablis winked at Lynton and said, "Wouldn't you like to know?"

**DON'T MISS THESE
CHABLIS LOUISE CHAVEZ
MYSTERIES**

*Chablis: Avenging Angel for the Forgotten
In the City of Lost Hope*

---

*Chablis and the Terrorist
Who Resurrected the Spirit of Che Guevara*

Pursuit

The Disappearance

AND THESE LYNTON ADVENTURES

Lynton Walks on Water

Lynton Curls Her Hair

Lynton and the Vampire at Taygaytay Manor

---

*Lynton Buys a Cell-Phone and Hears
the Voice of Doom*

---

*Lynton and the Ghosts at the Mansion
on Balete Drive*

www.ingramcontent.com/pod-product-compliance
Lightning Source LLC
Chambersburg PA
CBHW070624130626
46556CB00001B/459